U0025471

信天翁號一的獵鷹

The Albatross

作者 _Scott Lauder and Walter McGregor

譯者 _ 蔡裴驊

ABOUT THIS BOOK

For the Student

🎧 Listen to the story and do some activities on your Audio CD.
📺 Talk about the story.
⭐ Prepare for Cambridge English: Preliminary (PET) for schools.

For the Teacher

HELBLING e·ZONE A state-of-the-art interactive learning environment with 1000s
THE EDUCATIONAL PLATFORM of free online self-correcting activities for your chosen readers.

Go to our Readers Resource site for information on using readers and
downloadable Resource Sheets, photocopiable Worksheets, and Tapescripts.
www.helblingreaders.com

For lots of great ideas on using Graded Readers consult Reading Matters,
the Teacher's Guide to using Helbling Readers.

Level 5 Structures

Modal verb would	Non-defining relative clauses
I'd love to . . .	Present perfect continuous
Future continuous	Used to / would
Present perfect future	Used to / used to doing
Reported speech / verbs / questions	Second conditional
Past perfect	Expressing wishes and regrets
Defining relative clauses	

Structures from other levels are also included.

CONTENTS

Can you tell us a little about yourselves?

Scott

Scott I am doing a doctorate[1] in Education, so I don't get much time for hobbies. However, I do like to read fiction[2]. At the moment, I am reading Patrick O'Brian[3]. He wrote twenty-one books about Captain Aubrey, but I wish there were more.

Walter I love writing short stories, but my business keeps me very busy. I live in Scotland and I work there, too, so I often go hill-walking[4]. My other hobbies are playing guitar and sketching[5].

How did you two meet?

Walter We met at primary school[6] many years ago!

Have you written together before?

Scott Yes! We've written more than twenty stories so far.

1　doctorate [ˈdɑktərɪt] (n.) 博士學位
2　fiction [ˈfɪkʃən] (n.)（總稱）小說
3　Patrick O'Brian（1914－2000），英國作家，以描寫海戰和海軍
　　生活的《怒海爭鋒》系列小說聞名，此系列共 21 部小說。
4　go hill-walking 到山上健行
5　sketch [skɛtʃ] (v.) 素描

How does writing a book together work?

Walter

Walter Usually, one of us will have an idea and then we will talk about it. Because Scott lives in the UAE[7] and I am in Scotland[8], we chat on the computer a lot!

Does the book have a message?

Scott I think the book is partly about grief[9]. When someone important in our lives dies, we have to remember that person, but we also have to move forward[10].

Where did you get the idea for this story?

Walter Scott and I were sitting in a café next to the ocean. It was a cold, wet, windy night. As we looked out of the café's[11] window, we saw the lights of a boat in the Firth[12] of Clyde. What was the boat carrying, we wondered . . .

Any more stories in the future?

Scott **Walter** Lots!

---

6 primary school 小學
7 UAE 阿拉伯聯合大公國
   （United Arab Emirates）
8 Scotland ['skɑtlənd] (n.) 蘇格蘭
   （位於大不列顛島北部）
9 grief [grif] (n.) 悲傷
10 move forward 前進
11 café [kæ'fe] (n.) 咖啡廳
12 firth [fɜθ] (n.)（尤指蘇格蘭的）
   河口灣；港灣

1 The *Albatross* is the name of the cargo ship where different parts of the story are set. Look at this picture of a cargo ship and then use the words from the story in the box below to label the picture. Use a dictionary if necessary.

deck

stairwell

hold

hull

galley

a _____

b _____

c _____

d _____

e _____

2 These people all work on a ship. What do
they do? Write a definition with a partner.
Use a dictionary to help you.

captain

crew

engineer

3 What is an albatross? Work with a partner.
Write down some reasons why you think
the ship is called *The Albatross*.

4 Read and complete the following introductions to some of the characters in the story, using the words below. Then listen and check your answers.

a

My name's Molly Mundy and I'm 1_____ years old. I come from a small town called 2_____, which is on the east coast of the United States. I have a dog called 3_____. My hobbies include playing 4_____ and going for walks on the beach. I live with my father, who works for Haven Harbor 5_____. Apart from my dog, there are just 6_____ of us in our house, although my aunt often comes to visit in the 7_____: my dad thinks I need a babysitter and that makes me 8_____!

soccer
crazy
Police
Haven
two
Pip
afternoon
sixteen

b

My name's Leveros Andreas, but everyone calls me 1_____. I'm 2_____ years old and I work as a ship's 3_____. The voyage on *The Albatross* is my last one. After it finishes, I plan to 4_____. I want to go back to 5_____, buy a small boat and go fishing with my 6_____.

retire
sixty-five
brother
Levy
engineer
Greece

c

My name's **Carlos**. Who cares where I come from? I met Andre while we were both in 1_____. Andre is an idiot, but we always seem to 2_____ together. We met the captain of *The Albatross* in Malta. I didn't trust the captain then and I don't trust him now! Levy's okay and he's a good 3_____ to have on the 4_____, but he's old and wants everything to be perfect all the time.

ship
engineer
work
prison

d

My name's **Lieutenant Daniel Mundy**, but my friends call me 1_____. I have been a lieutenant for almost 2_____ years and I'm hoping to get a promotion soon. I work in Haven, but I live with my daughter, Molly, in a small house near 3_____ Bay. I'm a 4_____, since my wife died a few 5_____ ago. Having a wonderful daughter like Molly makes things easier.

years
Shell
Dan
four
widower

5 Read Exercise **4** again. Use the information to complete the sentences with the correct names.

a Pip belongs to _____ .

b _____ is Dan Mundy's daughter.

c The captain, Levy, Andre, and _____ work on *The Albatross*.

d _____ is Carlos's friend, but Carlos thinks he is an idiot.

e _____ is the ship's engineer on *The Albatross*.

f _____'s mother died a few years ago.

g _____ doesn't trust the captain.

h _____ and Carlos have been in prison.

6 Look at these action verbs from the story. What do they mean? Use a dictionary if necessary. When we do the action, do we usually use all of our body or part of our body or both? What do you think? Complete the table and check (✓) either "All," "Part" or "Both." Mime the actions with a partner.

Action	All	Part	Both
step			
lean			
nod			
tighten			
sprint			
glance			
shrug			
rush			
dash			
swallow			
wink			

7 Use some of the verbs from Exercise **6** to ask and answer these questions with a partner. Make questions for three other verbs and ask another pair.

(a) What would you do if you were in a hurry?

(b) What would you do if you agreed with someone?

(c) What would you do if you wanted to look at something quickly?

(d) What would you do if you were eating?

(e) What would you do if you didn't know the answer?

(f) What would you do if you were telling a joke?

8 Use the words below to complete these sentences.

> nodded
> stepped
> sprinted
> swallow

(a) Levy _____ forward but then jumped back. It wasn't a rat at his feet. It was an apple core.

(b) The captain _____ slowly. "Of course," he replied. "You're right."

(c) Levy felt thirsty. He tried to _____, but couldn't. Molly filled a glass of water for him.

(d) Pip gave Molly a quick look and _____ down the hill toward Shell Bay: his favorite place.

9 Look at the pictures below. What can you see? Tell a friend.

"But that's impossible"

The Albatross wasn't the most beautiful ship in the world, but Leveros Andreas didn't care. He was the ship's engineer[1] and everybody knew him as Levy. At sixty-five and after almost fifty years at sea, this was his final voyage[2]. He couldn't wait to retire[3] and use the money he had saved to buy a house in his home town of Nikiti, in Greece.

He and the other two members of the crew[4] were sailing toward the harbor[5] town of Haven with their cargo[6] of televisions. This was Levy's first time on The Albatross, but not his first time to visit Haven. Years before, when his wife was still alive, he had visited the little harbor town on the east coast of the United States with her. Those were happy years.

Levy looked at the gold watch that his wife had given him for his 40th birthday. "1:14!" he said.

Usually, he tried to be in bed by twelve; but Herman, the ship's cat, was missing.

---

1 engineer [ˌɛndʒəˈnɪr] (n.) 輪機員；機械工
2 voyage [ˈvɔɪɪdʒ] (n.) 航海
3 retire [rɪˈtaɪr] (v.) 退休
4 crew [kru] (n.) 全體機員
5 harbor [ˈhɑrbɚ] (n.) 港口；海港
6 cargo [ˈkɑrgo] (n.) 貨物

There was a storm coming and he was worried. "I'll murder[1] that cat when I find him!" he said, shaking his head.

There was only one more place to check: the cargo deck[2]. He began climbing down the stairs to the lowest deck. He had almost reached[3] the bottom step when he stopped. There, in front of him, the door to the cargo room lay[4] half open. It was dark inside. Normally, the door was locked for security[5] reasons. Levy thought about going to tell the captain immediately, but then he thought about Herman.

"Hermaaaan! Hey, Hermaaaan," Levy called from the door of the hold[6]. "Are you in there?"

He pulled out his flashlight[7]. "Hermaaaaan!" Levy called again.

The flashlight shined only a few feet through the door and into the darkness, but Levy didn't really want to go any farther. The truth was he was frightened of rats[8]. This was one of the reasons why he liked Herman.

Levy stood still. The ship was beginning to rise and fall more quickly now: the storm was getting closer.

"Herrrrr-maaaaaan, where are you?" Levy called out.

The captain's orders[9] were that no one was allowed[10] to go into the cargo hold but Levy had to find Herman. Hesitantly[11], Levy stepped forward[12] but he touched something with his foot. He jumped back and looked down. An apple core[13] lay at his feet. At least it wasn't a rat.

---

1 murder [ˈmɝdɚ] (v.) 謀殺   3 reach [ritʃ] (v.) 到達
2 deck [dɛk] (n.) 甲板   4 lie [laɪ] (v.) 呈……狀態（三態：lie; lay; lain）

"Andre!" thought Levy.

Andre was always leaving these things lying around. He pictured Andre's face. "Large" and "stupid" were the words that immediately came into his mind. Andre and his friend, Carlos, were his two crewmates[14]. Although it wasn't easy on a small ship, Levy tried to stay away from them as much as possible.

"I should get out of here," he thought. "That crazy cat will have to find his own way out: I need to go and tell the captain about this door."

"Kkkkeeeeeeeeew!" The sound came from somewhere in the darkness.

"Keeeeew! Keeeeeeew!"

The sound

- What do YOU think makes this sound?

"What was that?" he whispered[15] to himself.

He shined his flashlight into the darkness and moved toward the sound. The sound came again, only louder.

---

5 security [sɪˋkjʊrətɪ] (n.) 安全

6 hold [hold] (n.) 貨艙

7 flashlight [ˋflæʃ͵laɪt] (n.) 〔美〕手電筒

8 rat [ræt] (n.) 鼠

9 order [ˋɔrdɚ] (n.) 命令

10 allow [əˋlaʊ] (v.) 允許

11 hesitantly [ˋhɛzətəntlɪ] (adv.) 遲疑地

12 forward [ˋfɔrwəd] (adv.) 向前

13 core [kor] (n.) 果核

14 crewmate [ˋkru͵met] (n.) 工作同仁

15 whisper [ˋhwɪspɚ] (v.) 低聲說

Hundreds of boxes were piled[1] high on both sides of him; but there was a clear path[2] through them, like a river through a canyon[3]. Levy's mouth fell open[4]. At the far end of the hold, a light came from a half-open door.

"But that's impossible," he said. "There are no other rooms in the cargo hold."

But there was another room and there was another light and it was drawing[5] Levy forward like a moth[6] toward a lamp.

1 pile [paɪl] (v.) 堆積
2 path [pæθ] (n.) 小徑
3 canyon [ˋkænjən] (n.) 峽谷
4 the mouth falls open 吃驚得目瞪口呆
5 draw [drɔ] (v.) 吸引
　（三態：draw; drew; drawn）
6 moth [mɔθ] (n.) 蛾

2

"We have a problem"

Outside the room, Levy stopped. He could feel his heart beating[7] hard. He switched off[8] his flashlight and leaned[9] his head through the narrow doorway[10]. The first thing he saw was a large sheet[11] covering something. He stepped into the room. There were sheets everywhere.

With one hand he reached forward and, taking the nearest sheet, he pulled it off.

A beautiful falcon[12] with shining eyes stared[13] back at him from its cage.

"What on earth[14] . . .?" he said and reached for the other sheets.

Under each one, there were more birds. In all, Levy counted[15] nearly forty cages with one and sometimes two falcons in each. He was furious[16]. These birds were special. There were laws to protect[17] them from men like Andre. He thought about[18] the police. "If they find the birds, it'll mean trouble for all of us. I need to see the captain."

7　beat [bit] (v.) 擊；打
　　（三態：beat; beat; beat, beaten）
8　switch off 關掉
9　lean [lin] (v.) 傾身；傾斜（三態：
　　lean; leaned, leant; leaned, leant）
10　doorway [ˋdor͵we] (n.) 出入口
11　sheet [ʃit] (n.) 一張（紙）；一大塊（布）
12　falcon [ˋfɔlkən] (n.) 隼；獵鷹

13　stare [stɛr] (v.) 盯；凝視
14　what on earth
　　〔表驚訝〕這到底是怎樣
15　count [kaʊnt] (v.) 計算
16　furious [ˋfjʊərɪəs] (a.) 狂怒的
17　protect [prəˋtɛkt] (v.) 保護
18　think about 考慮

Picking up the nearest cage, he walked out of the hold and back up the stairs to the captain's room. He knocked on the door and went straight in.

Inside, the captain was sitting at a small desk, his ear to a cell phone. His big body made the room seem even smaller than it was.

"What's going on?[1]" he asked sharply[2] when Levy walked in.

"I'm sorry to disturb you," replied Levy, "but I found this in the hold," and he held up the cage.

The captain stared at the falcon. "I'll call you back," he said into his cell phone.

His dark eyes turned back to Levy. "What were you doing in the hold?" he asked.

"I was looking for Herman," answered Levy, "and I found this. There are more than forty cages down there."

Silence. "It's Andre," Levy continued. "He's responsible[3]."

"Andre? What makes you think it's him?"

"I found an apple . . ."

". . . and that means it's Andre?" the captain asked, a strange smile on his face.

Levy didn't understand: this was serious. "Captain," he said, "these are rare birds[4]; we could all go to jail[5] for this."

The captain seemed lost in thought[6].

---

1 what's going on 怎麼回事
2 sharply [ˈʃɑrplɪ] (adv.) 嚴厲地
3 responsible [rɪˈspɑnsəbḷ] (a.) 負責任的

4 rare bird 稀有鳥類
5 go to jail 坐牢
6 lost in thought 陷入沉思

Levy spoke again. "Call the police," he said, "before they come onto the ship and find the birds for themselves."

The captain nodded[1] slowly. "Of course," he replied. "You're right." He moved around the table and put his arm around Levy's shoulder. "I'll call them. Don't worry, everything's going to be fine. Okay?"

Levy nodded. "Okay", he said, beginning to relax. "I'll take the bird to my room."

The captain nodded and Levy opened the door. "Thank you, captain," he said.

As soon as[2] the door was closed and Levy was gone, the captain quickly called someone on his cell phone.

"We have a problem," said the captain.

Levy was walking along the corridor[3] that led to his room. He wanted to put the falcon somewhere safe. All of a sudden[4] Herman ran past, tail in the air.

"Hey," shouted Levy. "Where are you going?"

But Herman didn't stop. He continued at full speed[5] and disappeared down the corridor.

Levy laughed to himself. "Unbelievable[6]! I thought birds were supposed to[7] be scared of[8] cats."

Then Levy heard a noise behind him. He turned around quickly. Carlos and Andre stood a few feet away, both of them staring coldly at him. They looked big and heavy in their overalls[9].

---

1 nod [nɑd] (v.) 點頭；點頭表示
2 as soon as 一……就……
3 corridor [ˈkɔrɪdə] (n.) 走廊
4 all of a sudden 突然地；出乎意料地
5 at full speed 以極高的速度或極大的力量

(10) "Going somewhere?" asked Carlos.

"To my room," replied Levy.

Carlos smiled. He looked at the cage and said, "You have something that isn't yours."

Levy felt threatened[10]. He was too old to fight these two big guys. He tried to think of a way to get past them.

"Do you know what time it is?" asked Andre suddenly.

Levy looked at his watch: almost 1:32 A.M. Suddenly, a sharp pain filled Levy's head and everything went dark for a second. When he opened his eyes he was lying on the floor, but he was still holding the cage.

"You should give Carlos the falcon, old man," Andre said threateningly from behind Carlos's shoulder.

Carlos pushed his face close to Levy's. When he spoke, the smell of his breath filled Levy's nose. "Don't make me hurt you, old man," he whispered, his green eyes shining.

6 unbelievable [ˌʌnbɪˈlivəbl̩] (a.) 令人難以置信的
7 be supposed to . . . 被認為應該……
8 be scared of . . . 害怕……
9 overalls [ˈovɚˌɔlz] (n.)〔複〕（寬大、有肩帶的）工裝褲
10 threatened [ˈθrɛtn̩d] (a.) 受到威脅的

"Captain . . . " cried out Levy, "Captain!"

In an instant[1], Carlos's hand was around Levy's throat; the other across his mouth. "Stupid old man . . . " whispered Carlos.

Andre grabbed[2] the cage and tried to tear[3] it from Levy's hand. The cage fell backward and crashed[4] against the stairs that led to the deck above. The door of the cage swung[5] open.

"Catch it!" shouted Carlos, reaching out an arm. But it was too late.

The falcon disappeared through the open door above them and into the night. A second later, the men turned back to Levy. Carlos's fists[6] tightened[7].

Andre knocked on the captain's door. Beside him, Carlos was rubbing[8] his fists.

"Come in."

The men stepped inside.

"Well?" asked the captain.

Carlos and Andre looked at one another. "We had a slight[9] problem," said Carlos.

The captain stood up. "I know you had a problem!"

"Levy let the bird go," Andre lied.

The captain slammed[10] his hand on the desk. "That's one thousand dollars lost! You idiots!"

Andre looked at the floor, but Carlos's eyes blazed[11].

"Where is he?" continued the captain. "Where did you put him?"

"Don't worry, we took care of[12] him," replied Carlos.

"We gave him a bath," laughed Andre like a child. "Man overboard[13]!"

The captain sat down again and looked out of the small window. A black sky greeted him. The old man was never part of their plans and now he was dead. Fine! But if the police found his body quickly they would be in trouble. The police would know that the old man hadn't drowned[14].

"Don't worry. We've seen the last of him[15]," said Carlos, reading the captain's thoughts[16].

"I hope so," the captain said. "I certainly hope so."

---

1 in an instant 頃刻間
2 grab [græb] (v.) 攫取；抓取
3 tear [tɛr] (v.) 扯掉
   （三態：tear; tore; torn）
4 crash [kræʃ] (v.) 碰撞
5 swing [swɪŋ] (v.) 搖擺
   （三態：swing; swung; swung）
6 fist [fɪst] (n.) 拳頭
7 tighten ['taɪtn̩]
   (v.) 使變緊
8 rub [rʌb] (v.) 摩擦

9 slight [slaɪt] (a.) 輕微的；微小的
10 slam [slæm] (v.) 猛烈抨擊
11 blaze [blez] (v.) 閃耀
12 take care of 處理
13 overboard ['ovɚ,bord]
    (adv.)（自船上）落水
14 drown [draʊn] (v.) 淹死
15 see the last of sb/sth
    最後一次見到；再也不會見到
16 read sb's thoughts 讀出某人的心思

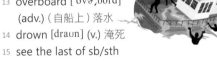

3

"A falcon"

🎧 13 Sixteen-year-old Molly Mundy stood beside her bed in a long, white shirt and rubbed her eyes. Her hair was a mess[1], and she felt horrible. A storm had woken her up at 3 A.M., and she hadn't fallen asleep[2] again for ages[3].

When she looked at her alarm clock, she groaned[4]. Today was Monday, Memorial Day[5] Monday, and she was wide awake[6] at exactly 7 A.M. She turned and looked at Pip who was watching her with excited eyes.

"Why did I forget to close my bedroom door last night?" she asked herself.

Pip was her dog and she loved him . . . except when he came into her room and woke her up with a cold, wet nose pressed[7] against her face.

She pulled open the curtains and looked outside. The air was clear and there was almost no wind.

"I guess I have no excuse, huh?" she asked Pip.

Watching his wagging[8] tail, she slipped on[9] a pair of jeans and pushed her dark hair under her old New York Cosmos cap.

Cap

- Do you know what New York Cosmos is?
  Do some research on the Internet to find out.

- Why do you think Molly has a New York Cosmos cap?

- Do you have a special cap or T-shirt? Tell a friend.

(14) "Okay," Molly said. "Let's go."

Immediately, Pip was at her side, following her down the stairs and into the living room. She pulled on a pair of white sports shoes and called into the kitchen.

"I'm taking Pip over to Shell Bay[10]," she said.

"Did you have your breakfast?" her father called back.

"Um . . . Won't be long," replied Molly.

"Hey, you got a key? I'm leaving for work soon," her father said.

"Yup[11]!"

"Have some breakfast when you come back, okay?"

---

1 mess [mɛs] (n.) 凌亂
2 fall asleep 睡著
3 for ages 很久；很長的時間
4 groan [gron] (v.) 呻吟
5 Memorial Day (美國) 陣亡將士
   紀念日 (五月的最後一個星期一)
6 wide awake 完全清醒
7 press [prɛs] (v.) 壓擠
8 wag [wæg] (v.) 搖
9 slip on 迅速穿上
10 bay [be] (n.) 海或湖泊的灣
11 yup [jʌp] (adv.) 是啊 (yes 的變體)

(15) "Okay, bye," replied Molly, and with Pip pushing past her, she stepped out of the door.

Shell Bay lay to the north of her house, a wide C-shaped line of yellow sand that ran for three miles up the coast toward the harbor at Haven. It was a fifteen-minute walk from her house over the hills to the beach, but she loved going there. Others from Haven sometimes went there, too, but she guessed the beach would be empty at this time.

At the top of the hill, Molly turned and looked back. Her father waved[1] to her and she waved back. She watched him get in his car and leave for work. Soon, the car was out of sight[2], traveling north along Highway 12 to Haven.

Her dad worked for Haven Harbor Police and Molly often worried about him, just like her mother used to do[3]. After her mother died two years ago, Molly tried to help out as much as possible: making shopping lists, doing the housework, ironing her dad's shirts, those kinds of things. And walking Pip[4].

Pip gave Molly a quick look and sprinted[5] down the hill to the beach. Molly held on to her cap and ran, too. Soon, they were both walking beside the sparkling[6] water.

After a while, Molly picked up a stick[7] and was about to throw it when she saw a bird flying to the north.

---

1 wave [wev] (v.) 揮；揮手表示
2 out of sight 超出視野而看不見
3 used to do sth 過去常常做某事
  （但現在已經沒有了）
4 walk a dog 蹓狗
5 sprint [sprɪnt] (v.) 奮力而跑
6 sparkle [ˋspark!] (v.) 閃耀
7 stick [stɪk] (n.) 枯枝

🎧16 "A falcon," she whispered.

The bird flew overhead[1]. She followed it with her eyes, turning to watch until it was too small to see.

Then Molly threw the stick for Pip. It fell somewhere on the other side of an old tree trunk[2] that lay near the water. Immediately, Pip went running after it. When he reached the tree trunk, he leaped[3] over it and disappeared from sight.

Molly began walking slowly toward him, taking deep breaths[4] of the fresh morning air. A ship that was slowly moving in the direction of Haven caught her eye.

"Glad I wasn't on that," she thought, remembering the storm from last night.

Now Pip was barking loudly. She smiled. "He's lost the stick," she thought and began looking for another one. Then she saw it: something shiny in the sand. She reached down and picked it up. It was a watch, a gold watch. The time on it said 1:38. She turned it over. On the back, there was writing, but she couldn't understand it. "What language is that?" she wondered.

Pip was now barking madly.

"What's the matter with him[5]?" She could just see his tail from behind the large tree trunk. "What is he so excited about?"

---

1 overhead [ˋovɚˋhɛd]
　(adv.) 在上頭；高高地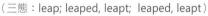
2 trunk [trʌŋk] (n.) 樹幹
3 leap [lip] (v.) 跳躍
　（三態：leap; leaped, leapt; leaped, leapt）
4 take deep breaths 深呼吸
5 what's the matter with sb 某人是怎麼了

She could see his head above the tree trunk now. He was running around, but his eyes were fixed on something behind the tree trunk.

Molly came closer . . . She stood and stared in horror[1].

An old man lay against the side of the tree trunk, his face to the sky. Molly turned and ran as fast as she could back along the beach. Pip was at her heels[2].

Molly

- What four things does Molly see or find that are linked to the first part of the story?

1 in horror 處在驚駭中
2 heel [hil] (n.) 腳後跟
3 pour [por] (v.) 傾注；傾瀉
4 cabin [ˋkæbɪn] (n.) 艙
5 broad [brɔd] (a.) 寬闊的
6 laptop [ˋlæptɑp]
　 (n.) 筆記型電腦

7 opposite [ˋɑpəzɪt] (prep.) 在對面
8 deliver [dɪˋlɪvɚ] (v.) 遞送
9 shame [ʃem] (n.) 憾事
10 distress call 求救電話；遇險電話
11 coast guard 海岸防衛隊

"There's something you need to see"

18   Morning sunshine was pouring[3] in through the cabin's[4] only window. Its yellow light fell on the captain's broad[5] back and his black uniform. With his laptop[6] open in front of him, he sat silently with his eyes on the screen. Andre and Carlos were sitting opposite[7] him. They were watching every move of his face.

It was the morning after the storm and the ship was sailing calmly on a sea of blue. They were near Haven now. In a few hours they could deliver[8] the birds and get their money.

"That was a good storm last night," said Andre, to no one in particular. "Shame[9] our engineer didn't enjoy it!"

Carlos looked at Andre coolly.

Andre smiled, showing a row of brown teeth. "Relax!" he said. "I know the story: the old man was sick. He fell over the side. We tried to save him, but we couldn't reach him . . . Then the captain made a distress call[10] to the Coast Guard[11]."

"Be quiet! Both of you," said the captain. "If the police find him now, we'll spend the next twenty years in prison. Think about THAT!" His words hung in the air for several moments.

 He switched off his laptop just as his cell phone rang. He answered it and at once[1] began shouting.

Andre leaned over to Carlos. "Hopper?" he whispered.

Carlos nodded.

"Wait," the captain told the caller. He stared at Andre and Carlos. "Go on deck and keep watch."

Andre and Carlos stood up and left the cabin. Behind them, they could hear the call with Hopper continue. Andre whistled happily as he climbed the stairs to the deck.

Carlos, however, was far from happy. He didn't like the way the captain spoke to him; but most of all, he didn't like the way the money, the $60,000 for the falcons, was divided[2]. Why should the captain get fifty percent? Why should he and Andre each get twenty-five percent? Up on deck, he was still deep in thought[3] when Andre pushed the powerful binoculars[4] in front of his face.

"There's something you need to see," he said, pointing to a nearby beach.

Carlos took the binoculars. "I don't believe it . . ." he said.

---

1 at once 立刻
2 divide [də`vaɪd] (v.) 分；分開
3 deep in thought 深思；沉思

4 binoculars [bɪ`nɑkjələz]
〔複〕(n.) 雙筒望遠鏡

"Captain's not going to like this," said Andre.

Like green flames[5], Carlos's eyes turned on him. "I told you to put him in chains[6]. Did you?"

Andre stared stupidly at Carlos. "There was some old rope . . ." he began to reply.

"Did you take out his ID[7]?"

Andre said nothing, but a look of panic[8] crossed his face.

"You idiot!'" hissed[9] Carlos.

"I forgot! There was too much to do. He was heavy and I couldn't . . ."

"Shut up!" Carlos shouted.

He had to think. Levy wasn't deep beneath them at the bottom of the ocean; he was lying on the beach like a sunbather[10]. Even worse, he still had his ID in his pocket. He knew he had to tell the captain and admit his mistake: he had told Andre to take care of Levy instead of doing it himself.

But right now, there was only one thing to do: they had to get the old man's body off the beach and hide it somewhere on the ship.

"Get the boat," Carlos said. "Bring the old man back on board and put his body in the hold."

Mouth open, Andre stood and stared.

"Get . . . the . . . boat," repeated Carlos slowly. "Now!"

---

5 flame [flem] (n.) 火焰
6 put sb in chains 將某人上鐐銬
7 ID 身分證明 (= identification)
8 panic [ˋpænɪk] (n.) 恐慌
9 hiss [hɪs] (v.) 發出嘶嘶聲
10 sunbather [ˋsʌn͵beðɚ] (n.) 日光浴者

5

"I'm sorry, Dad"

For hours, the police had gone up and down the beach searching for the body, but they had found nothing.

Molly looked toward the trail[1] that led over the hill. One after the other, the officers disappeared over the top of the hill. The last to vanish[2] were the two paramedics[3] who were carrying the empty stretcher[4].

In front of her, staring out at the ocean, her father stood on the beach in his gray harbor police shirt and pants. The hat that he was wearing made him seem even taller and thinner.

"I'm sorry, Dad," Molly finally said, taking his hand and looking up at him.

She didn't know what else to say. There had been a body. She had seen an old man lying dead on the sand. But now that body wasn't there. It had disappeared . . . it didn't make sense[5].

"It's not your fault," he said. "I . . . I haven't been there for you[6], not really." He looked down at her, "Not after Mom died." His eyes were soft and kind. "Anyway, I was thinking of taking a few days off work . . . going to the Big Apple[7]." He smiled. "We could see a show and stay at Grandma and Grandpa's."

Molly smiled, too. Her father was born in Haven, but her mother came from New York; and her grandparents still lived there, in the same house on Riverside Drive that her mother was born in. She loved visiting the Big Apple, especially Broadway[8]. She missed that. She also missed staying with her grandparents. Since her mother's death, she and her father hadn't stayed there once.

But the reason for the trip wasn't hard to guess. It was because of today. She guessed that her father thought the "body on the beach" was a cry for attention, that she imagined the whole thing. She didn't blame[9] him.

She squeezed[10] his hand.

"Listen, I have to go back to the office," he said gently[11]. "But I'll be back home around five, okay?"

"Yeah," said Molly, nodding. "Okay."

"You got practice[12] today?"

---

1 trail [trel] (n.) 小道
2 vanish [ˈvænɪʃ] (v.) 消失
3 paramedic [ˌpærəˈmɛdɪk] (n.) 醫護人員
4 stretcher [ˈstrɛtʃɚ] (n.) 擔架
5 make sense 有道理
6 be there for you 待在你身邊

7 Big Apple〔俚〕紐約市
8 Broadway [ˈbrɔd‚we] (n.) 百老匯
9 blame [blem] (v.) 責備
10 squeeze [skwiz] (v.) 緊握
11 gently [ˈdʒɛntlɪ] (adv.) 溫和地
12 practice [ˈpræktɪs] (n.) 練習

Molly shook her head. Haven High was district[1] soccer[2] champion[3] and Molly was the girls' team captain. "That was yesterday," she said.

"Yesterday . . ." Her father nodded. "Of course."

"What about the watch?" Molly asked.

"The watch?"

Molly pulled the watch from the back pocket of her jeans.

Her father glanced[4] at it. With his hand on her shoulder, they turned around and began walking toward the start of the trail.

"Well," said her father, "I guess somebody dropped it. Why don't you keep it for now and we'll put an ad[5] in Marty's store window?"

Molly turned the watch over in her hands. "The inscription[6] is in Russian[7] . . . or something," she said.

Her father, however, wasn't paying attention. Instead, he was looking out at the ocean. He was still looking there when Molly saw the falcon from earlier in the day. Now it was just above the top of the hill in front of them.

"Dad . . ." she said. But as soon as she said it, the bird dropped out of sight and was gone.

"Hmmm?" asked her father, turning toward her "What?"

"Oh, nothing," replied Molly.

1 district ['dɪstrɪkt] (n.) 地區；行政區
2 soccer ['sɑkɚ] (n.) 足球
3 champion ['tʃæmpɪən] (n.) 冠軍
4 glance [glæns] (v.) 一瞥；掃視
5 put an ad 刊登啟示
6 inscription [ɪn'skrɪpʃən] (n.) 刻印文字
7 Russian ['rʌʃən] (n.) 俄文

They walked on in silence. Her father put his arm around Molly and pulled her close to him.

"Is Aunt Ellie coming over today?" Molly asked.

Aunt Ellie was her father's older sister. Her father didn't like Molly being in the house by herself[1], too young, he said, so Aunt Ellie usually came later in the afternoon and stayed a few hours.

Her father nodded.

"But Dad, I'm sixteen. I don't need a babysitter[2]."

Her father smiled. "You're still my little girl."

That made Molly want to scream[3], but instead she ran ahead to the top of the hill.

In the distance, above the sound of the waves and the wind, the falcon's call rang out[4].

As soon as she got home, Molly went up to her room, with Pip following closely behind her.

On her bed, she read the name on the back of the watch again: "L-e-v-e-r-o-s." She thought again about the body on the beach. She had no idea[5] why, but she felt there was a connection[6]. She looked at Pip: the body's disappearance[7], and the words on the watch were of no interest to him at all. Instead, he was curled up[8] at the foot of the bed, his eyes already beginning to close. She smiled.

---

1 by oneself 獨自
2 babysitter [ˈbebɪ,sɪtɚ] (n.) 保姆
3 scream [skrim] (v.) 尖叫
4 ring out 響起
5 have no idea 不知道
6 connection [kəˈnɛkʃən] (n.) 關連
7 disappearance [ˌdɪsəˈpɪrəns] (n.) 消失

25   Her aunt Ellie was not coming until later in the afternoon and Molly didn't have school or soccer practice to go to. She had plenty of[9] time to do a little research before she had breakfast and did some chores[10] around the house.

    She switched on her laptop. She typed[11] the words from the back of the watch into Google translator[12]. A moment later, the translation appeared. She repeated the words slowly: "To my darling Leveros 'Levy' Andreas. All my love, K."

    The watch was a present from someone. It meant that the old man might be someone's grandfather, someone's uncle, or even someone's husband . . .

Information

- When you want to find information where do you look or what do you do? Check (✓).

  ☐ encyclopedia[13]   ☐ library
  ☐ Internet   ☐ newspaper
  ☐ ask an adult[14] or teacher

---

8 curl up 蜷作一團
9 have plenty of . . . 有很多⋯⋯
10 chores [tʃorz] (n.) 〔複〕家庭雜務
11 type [taɪp] (v.) 打字

12 translator [træns`letɚ] (n.) 翻譯機
13 encyclopedia [ɪnˌsaɪklə`pidɪə] (n.)
    百科全書
14 adult [ə`dʌlt; `ædʌlt] (n.) 成年人

6

"He's nervous . . . but the question is: why?"

Lieutenant Daniel Mundy had just spent two useless[1] hours on a beach near his home looking for a dead body. After the search, he had returned to the office and written a report. Then he had gone to the police cafeteria[2] for a late lunch.

He was having coffee, his first of the day, when his boss came to his table. "A cargo ship has just come in, Dan," his boss had said.

In reply, Mundy had felt like saying, "get someone else to check it," but he hadn't. It was part of his job.

Now it was 2:40 P.M. and he was standing below deck, documents[3] in one hand, flashlight in the other, carrying out[4] his usual inspection[5] of cargo. But a voice in his head was growing louder and louder all the time. Something about the hold and this man's behavior was not right . . .

He turned to the man who was escorting[6] him. "How many TVs are you carrying?" he asked, switching on the flashlight.

(27) "Sorry?" asked the captain.

The noise from the ship's engines and the generators[7] was loud and it was difficult to hear anyone unless they shouted. Lieutenant Mundy repeated his question and shined the flashlight through the door of the hold. Box after box greeted him as he moved his flashlight around the room.

"Eight hundred and fifteen," the captain replied, standing stiffly[8] at the door.

Lieutenant Mundy nodded slowly.

"That's all," the captain added.

"There it was again: something in the man's voice that was . . . odd," thought Lieutenant Mundy. "I see," he said, switching off his flashlight.

Lieutenant Mundy stepped past *The Albatross's* captain. "Are you sure this is all you have?" he asked, taking the customs[9] documents from his pocket. He kept his eyes fixed on the man's heavy face.

"You've seen all of the ship," replied the captain.

"That doesn't mean I've seen everything, does it?" Lieutenant Mundy asked. He smiled, but the captain did not return it.

"He's nervous," Lieutenant Mundy thought, "but the question is: why?"

---

1 useless [ˈjuslɪs] (a.) 沒有用的
2 cafeteria [ˌkæfəˈtɪrɪə] (n.) 自助餐廳
3 document [ˈdɑkjəmənt] (n.) 公文
4 carry out 執行
5 inspection [ɪnˈspɛkʃən] (n.) 檢查
6 escort [ˈɛskɔrt] (v.) 陪同
7 generator [ˈdʒɛnəˌretə] (n.) 發電機
8 stiffly [ˈstɪflɪ] (adv.) 僵硬地
9 customs [ˈkʌstəmz] (n.)〔複〕海關

He began filling in[1] the documents. Beside[2] the word Cargo, he wrote "TVs"; next to Number, he wrote "815."

"So, how long will you be staying in Haven?" he asked.

"A few days. Two perhaps."

Lieutenant Mundy nodded. He studied the captain's face. Experience[3] was a good teacher. After twenty years of working in Haven Harbor Police, Dan Mundy had met all kinds of people. Sometimes the lies they told were for stupid reasons, but most of the time people lied because they were breaking the law[4].

"How many are in the crew?" he asked.

The captain stood as still as a statue[5]. "Myself and three others. But as you probably know, the engineer was sadly lost."

Lieutenant Mundy stared at the man. "What did you say?" he asked.

"We lost a man at sea[6] . . . I've already reported it to the Coast Guard."

"When?" asked Lieutenant Mundy.

"Last night, around 3 A.M."

When Lieutenant Mundy had arrived at the office that morning, it had been quiet. Today was Memorial Day and reports from other agencies[7] such as the Coast Guard took longer than usual to reach his desk. Even so, he was angry: he should have known about this sooner.

Pictures of Molly telling him over and over that she had seen a body on the beach filled his head.

"I see. I'm sorry to hear that. Did you know him well?"

"No," replied the captain, "hardly at all[8]. Our regular[9] engineer became sick just before the voyage started so . . . bad luck, eh?"

"What was the new engineer's name?"

"Eh . . . Leveros Andreas," replied the captain, "but we called him Levy. Nice man . . . very sad."

---

1 fill in 填寫
2 beside [bɪˋsaɪd] (prep.) 在……旁邊
3 experience [ɪkˋspɪrɪəns] (n.) 經驗
4 break the law 違反法令
5 statue [ˋstætʃʊ] (n.) 雕像

6 at sea 在大海上
7 agency [ˋedʒənsɪ] (n.) 行政機構
8 hardly at all 幾乎沒有
9 regular [ˋrɛgjələ] (a.) 定期的；
     固定的

Lieutenant Mundy nodded. "Was he young?"

The captain shook his head. "He was an old guy, Greek . . . I gave the details[1] already."

"Right," said Lieutenant Mundy, "I'm sure you did. Well, I think everything is fine here. Can you just sign[2] this, please?"

He passed the customs documents to the captain. The captain signed and returned them.

"I hope you have a pleasant time in Haven," Lieutenant Mundy said.

A faint[3] smile crossed the captain's face.

Molly reached for the home phone and picked it up.

"Hi honey," said Molly's father into his cell phone. "You busy?"

"No, just making dinner. Aunt Ellie is here."

"Great! Listen . . . the reason I'm calling is I want to apologize[4] about earlier . . . I don't know what's going on, but I think you were right."

"About what?" asked Molly.

"I think you did see someone on the beach. In fact, I'm sure of it. I just wanted to say I was sorry . . ."

"It's okay," Molly interrupted[5]. "It was kind of weird[6]. I mean one minute there was a body on the beach and the next minute, it's gone."

"Yeah, well, anyway. I just wanted to say I was sorry, okay?"

"Okay," replied Molly.

"By the way, did you say the person that you saw was pretty old?"

"Yeah," replied Molly, "probably near seventy. I mean with his gray hair and . . ."

"Right, that's all I wanted to know. See you later . . ." Her father was about to end the call, but Molly stopped him.

"Dad, wait," she said. "Do you think the watch belonged to him?"

"What watch?" he asked.

"The one I found on the beach this morning. You know, the one with the writing on the back. I found out what the inscription said: it's Greek. The watch belonged to someone called Andreas . . ."

---

1 detail [ˈditel] (n.) 細節；詳情
2 sign [saɪn] (v.) 簽（名）
3 faint [fent] (a.) 微弱的
4 apologize [əˈpɑləˌdʒaɪz] (v.) 道歉
5 interrupt [ˌɪntəˈrʌpt] (v.) 打斷講話
6 weird [wɪrd] (a.) 奇怪的；神祕的

7

"We bring the birds; he brings the cash"

The three men were sitting around a table in the ship's galley[1]. Only ten minutes had passed since the visit from the harbor police, but the captain of *The Albatross* had already forgotten the lieutenant's name.

When Carlos asked him about what had happened, the captain shrugged[2]: "The cop[3] asked a few questions, nothing to worry about," he said.

"So what happens now?" asked Carlos.

"Hopper," said the captain, "wants me to meet him later in town. The deal[4] is arranged for 4 A.M. We bring the birds; he brings the cash[5]."

Hopper was the man who bought the animals that they smuggled[6], and he only wanted to deal with[7] the captain. That made Carlos mad. Why should the captain get $30,000? Was his job twice as[8] dangerous? Was he twice as smart?

"There must be some way to make Hopper trust me," thought Carlos. "I need to get Hopper's number, or . . ." Slowly, another plan began to form in his head.

---

1 galley [ˈgælɪ] (n.)（船上的）廚房
2 shrug [ʃrʌg] (v.) 聳肩
3 cop [kɑp] (n.)〔口〕警察
4 deal [dil] (n.) 交易
5 cash [kæʃ] (n.) 現金
6 smuggle [ˈsmʌgl] (v.) 走私
7 deal with 處理
8 twice as . . . 兩倍的……

Andre finished eating his apple and wiped his mouth with his sleeve. "What about the police?" he asked, moving his eyes from the captain's face to Carlos's.

"What about them?" asked the captain.

"Are they coming back?"

"Perhaps. I showed them the hold and our passports[1], but they'll want to check all of our stories about Levy," replied the captain, getting to his feet[2].

"Why are you going to see Hopper by yourself?" asked Carlos suddenly[3].

For a moment[4], the captain was too surprised to say anything and a silence fell. Then he let out[5] a deep breath and smiled coldly[6]. "It's very simple: Hopper is a very nervous man; and you, my friend, make him even more nervous."

Although it was late afternoon, the sun was still shining brightly and the air was hot. Molly, however, was walking beneath the trees. She was enjoying the coolness of the shade[7], the sharp[8] smell of pine[9] trees, and the sight of Pip chasing[10] birds.

---

1 passport [`pæs,port] (n.) 護照；通行證
2 get to one's feet 站起來
3 suddenly [`sʌdn̩lɪ] (adv.) 突然地
4 for a moment 一會兒；片刻

5 let out 放出
6 coldly [`koldlɪ] (adv.) 冷淡地
7 shade [ʃed] (n.) 陰涼處
8 sharp [ʃɑrp] (a.) (味道) 強烈的

She was on the narrow path[11] that led around the hills and into Haven. Earlier, Aunt Ellie had noticed that they were running out of[12] dog food.

"I'll go," Molly had said immediately. "I need the walk."

Below the tallest tree in the woods, she looked at her watch. It was nearly 4:30.

"I hope the pet store is open," she thought. "After all[13] it is Memorial Day. If it's shut[14], I'll go to Marty's," Molly thought. "I can get some cans[15] of meat in there, at least."

Marty's was the local drugstore[16], and it never closed.

Pip was now at her side and a few moments later, they both stepped out of the woods and onto Haven's Main Street.

"Don't worry," she said to Pip. "We're nearly there."

She reached out to put a leash[17] on Pip. He, however, turned his head sharply and went running after two seagulls[18] on a nearby low wall. They watched him come noisily toward them. Then, stretching their long wings, they rose lazily above the wall and rooftops.

Pip and Molly watched them fly toward the woods when suddenly they changed their course and dived away, heading[19] instead toward the open ocean.

9 pine [paɪn] (n.) 松樹
10 chase [tʃes] (v.) 追逐
11 path [pæθ] (n.) 小徑
12 run out of 用完
13 after all 畢竟
14 shut [ʃʌt] (v.) 打烊
　　（三態：shut; shut; shut）
15 can [kæn] (n.) 罐頭
16 drugstore [ˋdrʌɡ͵stor] (n.) 〔美〕藥房雜貨店
17 leash [liʃ] (n.) 狗鍊
18 seagull [ˋsi͵ɡʌl] (n.) 海鷗
19 head [hɛd] (v.) 向……出發

(35) Puzzled[1], Molly looked to see why. Out of the sun, a dark shape came. She narrowed her eyes. It was a falcon, perhaps the same one from the beach. Flying fast and low, it passed overhead. It then landed on the top of a warehouse[2] beside a ship that was in the dock[3].

Pip barked.

"Let's get you some food," she said.

A few moments later, they arrived outside the pet store. Molly tied Pip to the railing[4], and went inside.

In a building across the road from the pet store, Sergeant[5] Bergson moved back from the curtains and turned to Lieutenant Mundy. "Sir, you need to take a look at this."

"What is it?" Lieutenant Mundy asked, coming to the window.

He took the binoculars; and for a moment, he stopped breathing.

"What should we do, sir?"

"Get SWAT[6] here! Now!" roared[7] Dan Mundy.

Police

- Who are the police watching with the binoculars?

- What is SWAT? What do they do? Use the Internet to find out.

---

1 puzzled ['pʌzḷd] (a.) 困惑的   3 dock [dɑk] (n.) 碼頭
2 warehouse ['wɛr,haʊs] (n.) 倉庫   4 railing ['relɪŋ] (n.) 欄杆

"Murder wasn't part of the deal"

Inside the store, the usual smell of straw[8] and small animals greeted Molly, but there was no one behind the counter[9]. She took two cans of dog food from the shelf. "Should I just leave the money next to the cash register[10]?" she wondered.

Then she heard voices. They were coming from the back of the store. With the cans still in her hand, she stepped behind the counter. A door to another room was open slightly.

"Everything's fine," said a man's voice from behind the door. "We had a little problem, but everything's fine."

"A problem?" asked the other person.

Molly recognized the voice: it was Mr. Hopper's, the pet store owner.

"We had to bring him back to the ship. We'll dump[11] his body again once we get into deeper water . . ."

"I don't like it. I just don't like it. Murder wasn't part of the deal . . ." replied Mr. Hopper.

---

5 sergeant [ˈsɑrdʒənt] (n.) 警察小隊長；警官
6 SWAT 特種警察部隊；霹靂小組
   （Special Weapons And Tactics）
7 roar [ror] (v.) 吼叫

8 straw [strɔ] (n.) 稻草
9 counter [ˈkaʊntɚ] (n.) 櫃檯
10 cash register 收銀機
11 dump [dʌmp] (v.) 傾倒

"Shut up! You don't need to like it. I'll worry about Levy. You worry about paying me the $80,000."

Molly could hardly breathe. She had to get out of here. She had to tell her father. She had to explain what she had heard. She turned around.

A pair of green eyes stared straight at her.

"Little girls with big ears," said the man who stood in front of her, "might hear something they shouldn't."

For a second, Molly thought about rushing[1] past this man, but his heavy body filled the space between her and the front door completely. She took a step back.

The man didn't move or say a word, but Molly was scared[2]. It was his eyes, his green, narrow eyes. They were as hard and as dead as steel[3].

Molly felt her heart begin to beat faster. Through the window, she could see Pip outside by the railing. He was standing and watching the man's every move. His teeth were bared[4], and his ears were flat[5] against his head.

"I was just buying some dog food . . . for my dog," said Molly, trying to keep her breathing normal, trying to sound brave. She held up the two cans.

The man said nothing, but his green eyes continued to stare.

(38) "Do something!" shouted some part of Molly's brain.

She cast[6] her eyes around. Behind her, at the end of a short corridor, she saw there was another door. An exit? A storeroom[7]?

The man with the green eyes seemed to read her thoughts. Before Molly could move, his arm was up against the wall, blocking her way.

"Relax," he said, breathing into her face.

Bad situation[8]

- Have you ever been in a bad situation? Tell a friend.

"Who's there?" called a voice.

Molly turned as the half-open door swung sharply open. A heavy man in black pants and a black jacket stepped forward, followed by a pale-faced[9] Mr. Hopper.

"What are you doing here?" shouted the man in the black uniform.

---

1 rush [rʌʃ] (v.) 衝

2 scared [skɛrd] (a.) 吃驚的；嚇壞的

3 steel [stil] (n.) 鋼鐵

4 bared [bɛrd] (a.) 露出的

5 flat [flæt] (a.) 平的

6 cast [kæst] (v.) 投射（光線、視線）
（三態：cast; cast; cast）

7 storeroom ['stor‚rum] (n.) 儲藏室

8 situation [‚sɪtʃu'eʃən] (n.) 情況；處境

9 pale-faced ['pel'fest] (a.) 臉色蒼白的

53

The man with green eyes smiled. "Following you," he said calmly.

"What's going on?" asked Mr. Hopper. Molly and he were now both behind the counter. "Who's he? And what's she doing here?" he asked, jerking[1] a thumb at Molly.

The two men ignored[2] him. Instead, they stood eye to eye[3], a few feet apart[4]. From behind the counter, Molly had a good view of Pip. He was barking loudly, pulling at his leash and trying to get his head out of his collar[5].

"His name's Carlos," said the man in the black uniform, "and he was just leaving."

Carlos smiled again. "I don't think so," he said. "The captain and I have something to talk about."

"There's nothing we need to talk about," replied the captain.

"You're wrong," Carlos said calmly. "You see, I want you to explain the difference between $60,000 and $80,000."

"What's he talking about?" asked Hopper, leaning across the counter toward the two men.

Outside, Molly saw that Pip was no longer struggling[6] to get free. Instead, he was standing quietly, his tail moving from side to side happily. "That's strange," she thought.

"He's talking nonsense[7]," said the captain.

1 jerk [dʒɝk] (v.) 突然一動
2 ignore [ɪgˋnor] (v.) 忽視；不理會
3 eye to eye 正面對視（指衝突）
4 apart [əˋpɑrt] (adv.) 相隔兩地
5 collar [ˋkɑlɚ] (n.) 頸圈
6 struggle [ˋstrʌgl̩] (v.) 奮鬥；努力
7 nonsense [ˋnɑnsɛns] (n.) 胡說

Carlos's face changed. "I always knew you were a liar[1]," he said.

Suddenly Carlos moved toward the captain. He had a knife in his hand. Just in time, the captain raised[2] his arm and stopped Carlos's knife from plunging[3] into his chest. The captain grabbed Carlos's wrist; and the two men began fighting, crashing into shelves and smashing[4] into cages.

Out of the corner of her eye, Molly saw a gray uniform outside the store . . . Then everything happened at once. Carlos pushed the knife toward the captain's neck; Hopper screamed; the door at the back of the store exploded[5]; shouts filled the air; Hopper threw his hands up; the police threw the men to the ground; Molly jumped across the counter and into her father's arms. In an instant, it was over.

Molly was safely outside the store with a blanket around her shoulders, watching while Carlos, the captain and Hopper were handcuffed[6] and taken to three separate[7] police cars.

Her father put his arms around her and gave her a huge hug.

"I'm fine, Dad, honestly, I am," she said, while at the same time trying to stop Pip from jumping up and licking her face.

But her father noticed her hand was shaking: a typical symptom[8] of shock. "Let someone check you, okay? Just for me. It'll take two minutes, I promise."

Molly was too tired to argue⁹. "Okay," she said, handing Pip's leash to her father, "you win."

Her father smiled. They were almost at the steps of the ambulance, when she glanced over her shoulder.

The police cars that were carrying Carlos, Hopper and the captain were moving slowly up Main Street, but the crowd wasn't watching them. Instead, everyone was looking at something else, something in the sky. She stopped and looked up, too.

The sky was full of falcons. They all seemed to be coming from one ship in the harbor and they were moving in all directions at once.

1 liar [ˈlaɪɚ] (n.) 說謊者
2 raise [rez] (v.) 舉起
3 plunge [plʌndʒ] (v.) 刺進
4 smash [smæʃ] (v.) 猛撞
5 explode [ɪkˈsplod] (v.) 爆破
6 handcuffed [ˈhænd,kʌft] (a.) 戴上手銬的
7 separate [ˈsɛprɪt] (a.) 分隔的；個別的
8 symptom [ˈsɪmptəm] (n.) 症狀
9 argue [ˈɑrgju] (v.) 爭論

9

"He was dead!"

Molly sat on the edge of the bed in the back of the ambulance while the paramedic took her pulse[1]. From the open doors, she watched as more and more falcons rose into the sky.

"It's so strange," Molly said to her father. "Where do you think they are coming from?"

"I'm not sure," he replied, shielding[2] his eyes from the sun. "But I think it's something to do with the ship that I visited earlier: *The Albatross*."

"Is it difficult for you to breathe?" the paramedic asked Molly.

She shook her head.

Her father took out his phone and called a number. "Hi, Ellie, it's me," he said, and faintly[3] Molly could hear her aunt's voice in reply. Her father began explaining what had happened. Molly could imagine her aunt's face.

"No, she's fine . . ." her father was saying. "She's fine . . . she's fine."

1 pulse [pʌls] (n.) 脈搏
2 shield [ʃild] (v.) 擋避
3 faintly [ˈfentlɪ] (adv.) 微弱地

Molly smiled.

Her father listened for a second. "Yes, okay," he said.

A moment later, when the call ended, he put his phone away and turned to Molly. "Your Aunt Ellie's coming," he said.

Molly nodded.

The paramedic who had checked Molly spoke to her father. "She's had a nasty[1] fright[2]," he said. "But her blood pressure[3], breathing, and pulse are all fine."

"Told you!" said Molly.

"Good," said her father. "Because when Aunt Ellie arrives here, I want you to go back home with her; I'm going to the docks."

"But Dad!" cried Molly. "That's not fair."

Her father smiled. "You've had enough excitement for one day."

Standing on the docks beside *The Albatross*, megaphone[4] in hand, Lieutenant Mundy held up his left hand. He was signaling[5] to his men to wait. Situations like this always made him nervous. There were so many things that they didn't know. Would the third member of the crew give up[6] easily? Did he have a gun? Were there others on the ship? There was only one way to find out. They had to go on board[7].

"This is Lieutenant Mundy of Haven Harbor Police. Come out. We have the ship surrounded[8]," he said.

His voice boomed[9] through the speaker[10] and echoed[11] off the ship's steel hull[12]. He waited. No response[13]. He turned and waved his men forward. Immediately, six officers moved past him and began running along the narrow gangway[14] onto the ship, guns in hand. Almost as soon as they were on it, they began shouting.

"Get out!" they yelled. "Get on your knees[15]. Get on your knees."

Slowly, a pair of hands, then a head came out of one of the stairwells[16] that led below the deck. Finally, a tall man emerged[17], his hands high in the air. It was Andre. His face was white, his eyes staring.

"No!" Andre was shouting. "He was dead. He was dead!"

In a second, the harbor police surrounded him. They pushed Andre to the ground and handcuffed him, but still the man continued. "I saw him. I saw him. I saw him," he moaned[18].

Guess

- Who is Andre talking about?

1 nasty [ˈnæstɪ] (a.) 使人難受的
2 fright [fraɪt] (n.) 驚嚇
3 blood pressure 血壓
4 megaphone [ˈmɛɡəˌfon] (n.) 麥克風；大聲公
5 signal [ˈsɪɡnl̩] (v.) 以動作示意
6 give up 放棄
7 on board 在船上
8 surround [səˈraʊnd] (v.) 圍繞
9 boom [bum] (v.) 發出隆隆聲
10 speaker [ˈspikɚ] (n.) 喇叭
11 echo [ˈɛko] (v.) 回響
12 hull [hʌl] (n.) 船身
13 response [rɪˈspɑns] (n.) 回應
14 gangway [ˈɡæŋˌwe] (n.) 跳板；舷梯
15 get on one's knees 跪下
16 stairwell [ˈstɛrˌwɛl] (n.) 樓梯井
17 emerge [ɪˈmɝdʒ] (v.) 出現
18 moan [mon] (v.) 呻吟

61

(45)   "Lieutenant Mundy!" called Sergeant Bergson. He was at the bottom of the stairwell that Andre had come up. "You need to take a look at this."

Lieutenant Mundy stepped quickly into the stairwell and went below deck. Sergeant Bergson and two more officers were standing in front of the door to the hold. Although the lights inside it were switched on, it was still almost dark. Lieutenant Mundy switched on his flashlight and stepped through the doorway.

This time, the scene was very different. This time, the boxes were no longer in neat[1] rows.

"Looks like there's been a fight," he thought.

But that wasn't the biggest difference. There, at the end of the hold, beyond the messy[2] piles of boxes on the floor, lay a half-open door through which a bright light was shining. And now everything made sense to him. The hold was smaller than normal. He had been correct. The reason for that was simple. There was a false wall[3] that separated one part of the hold from the other.

He drew his gun and signaled silently for one of his men to go left and for one to go right. He, Sergeant Bergson, and the others moved slowly forward.

With every step closer, the men could see how much the false wall resembled[4] the real walls of the hold. It was made of thin wood, but painted exactly the same color as the real hold. In fact, without the door being open, no one would ever know the secret room was there.

---

1 neat [nit] (a.) 整齊的   3 false wall 假牆
2 messy [ˈmɛsɪ] (a.) 混亂的   4 resemble [rɪˈzɛmbl̩] (v.) 像；類似

（46） All four of them reached the false wall and lined up[1] with their backs against it. With his gun in his right hand, Lieutenant Mundy started a countdown with the fingers of his left hand . . . 3 . . . 2 . . . 1.

First Lieutenant Mundy followed by Sergeant Bergson and then the other two officers dashed[2] through the door, their bodies tense[3], their guns ready.

There, in the small room, among empty birdcages, lay the body of an old man, his face turned away from them, his clothes damp[4], his gray hair sticking to[5] his skull[6].

Lieutenant Mundy knelt down and reached for the man's wrist. He pressed his fingers to the main vein. The man's skin felt ice cold. Lieutenant Mundy began loosening[7] his fingers, preparing to drop the old man's wrist. But then he felt it, the faintest of pulses.

"Get an ambulance," he shouted. "He's still alive."

Old man

- Can you remember everything that happened to this old man? Go back to the text and check.

1 line up（使）整隊
2 dash [dæʃ] (v.) 急奔
3 tense [tɛns] (a.) 繃緊的
4 damp [dæmp] (a.) 潮濕的

10

"The shoes!"

Molly came to Haven Hospital for the first time when she was nine years old. She had fallen off her bike and landed badly. A cut[8] had appeared on her chin and bled[9] onto her new T-shirt. When she arrived home, her mother had wrapped[10] her in a yellow towel from the bathroom. Then, calmly, she had driven Molly to Haven Hospital. She could still remember her mother's warm hand around her; the yellow towel turning red; the hospital doors opening and the smell greeting her for the first time.

The next time she went to the hospital, the same smell greeted her. This time, her mother was having treatment[11] for her cancer[12]. Molly had tried to hold her breath[13] for as long as she could. It was a silly game. A month later, when her mother died, Molly had held her breath for two minutes.

Today, she was in the hospital once again, surrounded by the same familiar, sharp smell that she hated.

5 stick to . . . 黏在……上
6 skull [skʌl] (n.) 〔口〕腦袋；頭腦
7 loosen [ˈlusn̩] (v.) 鬆開
8 cut [kʌt] (n.) 傷口
9 bleed [blid] (v.) 流血
  （三態：bleed; bled; bled）
10 wrap [ræp] (v.) 包；裹
11 treatment [ˈtritmənt] (n.) 治療
12 cancer [ˈkænsɚ] (n.) 癌症
13 hold one's breath 摒住呼吸

She was in an elevator[1] climbing to the sixth floor. A nurse who was carrying charts[2] was standing in front of her, his face to the doors. Beside her, her father stood in his gray uniform, gun by his side. This time she and her father were on police business. This time, Molly wasn't holding her breath.

Smell

- Can you think of a place that has a particular smell? Tell a friend.

The elevator's doors opened and a tall woman, with long dark hair, stepped forward and introduced herself. "My name's Dr. Afreen. I believe you're here to see Mr. Andreas," she said and gave Molly a smile.

"That's right," replied Molly's father.

They began walking along the corridor.

"Has he said anything since he came in?"

"He's been unconscious[3] the whole time," replied Dr. Afreen.

1 elevator [ˈɛləˌvetɚ] (n.) 〔美〕電梯
2 chart [tʃɑrt] (n.) 圖表
3 unconscious [ʌnˈkɑnʃəs] (a.) 不省人事的

(49) Molly's father nodded. "That's okay. We know a little about him from one of the others on the ship. Seems Mr. Andreas was the engineer on board. He discovered his crew mates were trying to smuggle rare birds and threatened to call the police."

The doctor shook her head. "So they decided to kill him?"

"Yeah," replied Molly's father. "They threw him overboard, but he turned up[1] on the beach. That's when my daughter, Molly, saw him . . ."

"How terrible for you," the doctor said, her sparkling[2] hazel[3] eyes falling on Molly.

"They brought him back to the ship and put him in the hold. They were waiting until they were in deep water to throw him in the ocean again . . ." continued Molly's father.

"Awful[4]," said the doctor quietly.

"I just need Molly to formally identify him. Make sure that he was the man she saw on the beach. Is that okay?'

"Sure," said Dr. Afreen and she opened the door and led them into the room.

"It's him," said Molly quietly when she saw the old man in the bed.

"Are you absolutely[5] sure it's the old man you saw on the beach?" her father asked.

Molly nodded.

1 turn up 出現
2 sparkling [ˈspɑrklɪŋ] (a.) 放出火花的
3 hazel [ˈhezl] (a.) 淡褐色的
　（尤指眼睛的顏色）
4 awful [ˈɔful] (a.) 可怕的
5 absolutely [ˈæbsəˌlutlɪ] (adv.) 絕對地
6 be done here 完成 (= be finished)
7 regain [rɪˈgen] (v.) 恢復

68　The Albatross

"Okay," said Molly's father, putting an arm around her. "I think we are done here[6]. Thank you for your time."

"You're welcome," said Dr. Afreen, shutting the door and stepping out into the corridor once again with Molly and her father.

"I'll come back when Mr. Andreas has regained[7] consciousness[8]," said Molly's father, but just as Dr. Afreen was about to answer, an announcement[9] sounded: "Dr. Afreen, please report to Room 67. Dr. Afreen to Room 67, please."

She shrugged her shoulders. "Sorry, I've gotta[10] go," she said and she began hurrying down the corridor. "Nice meeting you," she said.

Molly and her father watched her go.

"She's nice," said Molly. "Don't you think?"

Her father smiled, but said nothing. They began walking toward the elevators again. Molly noticed that the hospital smell seemed even stronger in the corridors than in the patients'[11] rooms. Just then, her father's cell phone rang.

"Hello?" said her father. There was a pause[12] while he listened to the voice on the other end. "You gotta be kidding me[13]!" he said suddenly, almost shouting. "Never mind how it happened, we'll sort that out[14] later. Right now, we have to concentrate[15] on finding him . . ."

---

8 consciousness [ˈkɑnʃəsnɪs] (n.) 意識
9 announcement [əˈnaʊnsmənt] (n.) 宣布
10 gotta [ˈgɑtə]〔口〕= have got to
11 patient [ˈpeʃənt] (n.) 病患

12 pause [pɔz] (n.) 暫停；中斷
13 kidding me 跟我開玩笑
14 sort sth out 解決某事
15 concentrate [ˈkɑnsɛnˌtret] (v.) 集中

What was he talking about? What was happening?

" . . . and I want road blocks[1] on Highway 12 and I want CCTV footage[2] of the area . . ." continued her father.

Molly noticed a man coming along the corridor toward them. He was carrying a bouquet[3] of flowers so large that it covered most of his face. She didn't pay much attention to[4] him, but she did happen to glance at his feet. What she saw puzzled[5] her.

Her father's phone call ended and they continued walking to the elevator.

"Unbelievable," her father said angrily.

"What's up?" asked Molly as the elevator arrived.

Her father let out an angry sigh[6]. "It's Carlos. He was let out of the police station," he said, watching the elevator doors open.

"Carlos . . .? But how?" asked Molly.

They stepped into the elevator.

"A clerical error[7]. He was misidentified[8] and released[9] by mistake[10] . . ." replied her father, pressing the button for the floor that was marked 'G'. "He was in jail," he continued, "and he just walked out . . ."

The elevator doors began to close. Between the closing doors, the view of the corridor became thinner and thinner and thinner . . .

52   Suddenly, straight as a sword[11], Molly thrust[12] her arm between the closing doors. For a second, Molly's arm was crushed[13] painfully and she cried out. Then the doors reversed[14] their direction and once again, the corridor was fully visible.

"The shoes!" Molly said, rubbing her arm and stepping out of the elevator. "The man, that passed us in the corridor holding the big bouquet of flowers—he didn't have any laces[15] in his shoes . . ."

Her father looked at her as though she were talking nonsense.

"Like in jail," she said, "Like in jail!"

1   block [blɑk] (n.) 障礙（物）
2   footage [ˈfʊtɪdʒ] (n.)
   （影片的）連續鏡頭
3   bouquet [buˈke] (n.) 花束
4   pay attention to . . . 注意到⋯⋯
5   puzzle [ˈpʌzl] (v.) 使迷惑
6   sigh [saɪ] (n.) 嘆息
7   clerical error 辦事員的出錯
8   misidentify [ˌmɪsaɪˈdɛntəfaɪ]
   (v.) 識別錯誤

9   release [rɪˈlis] (v.) 釋放；豁免
10   by mistake 錯誤地
11   sword [sord] (n.) 劍
12   thrust [θrʌst] (v.) 塞；擠
   （三態：thrust; thrust; thrust）
13   crush [krʌʃ] (v.) 擠壓
14   reverse [rɪˈvɝs] (v.) 反轉
15   lace [les] (n.) 鞋帶

"If I am cursed, then he is lucky"

53 "If I were you, I wouldn't do that," said Lieutenant Mundy.

Two blazing green eyes turned and stared at the gun that was now pointing straight at them.

"Drop it," Lieutenant Mundy said in a low voice. "Now!"

Slowly, Carlos brought the pillow away from the old man's face. When the pillow was past the edge[1] of the bed, he released it. It fell from his hands and landed with a soft thud[2] beside the bouquet of flowers that already lay on the ground.

"Step away from him, nice and slow."

Carlos, eyes still fixed on the gun, moved a few feet away from the bed in which Levy lay. As he did so, he cast a glance at the window on the wall of the other side of the bed.

Lieutenant Mundy smiled. "I won't stop you . . ." he said, "although I should remind you that we are six floors up. "Now get on your knees and put your hands on your head. Now!"

Carlos's body became as tense as a spring[3]. But Lieutenant Mundy could read his thoughts. This man with green wolf-like eyes was calculating[4] his chances of attacking[5] him and getting the gun.

---

1 edge [ɛdʒ] (n.) 邊緣
2 thud [θʌd] (n.) 砰的一聲
3 spring [sprɪŋ] (n.) 彈簧
4 calculate [ˈkælkjəˌlet] (v.) 估計
5 attack [əˈtæk] (v.) 攻擊

"If you're a gambling[1] man," said Lieutenant Mundy calmly[2], "then go ahead and try . . ."

Reluctantly[3], Carlos dropped to one knee, and then two. He raised his hands and placed them on top of his head.

"Cross your legs behind you," ordered Lieutenant Mundy. "Do it!"

With his gun pointed steadily[4] at Carlos, Lieutenant Mundy reached for the handcuffs that he always carried in his belt.

As he did so, three hospital security officers[5] burst through[6] the door behind him. Within moments, Carlos was securely[7] handcuffed, and lying flat on the ground. The three security officers were standing over him waiting for the reinforcements[8] that Lieutenant Mundy had called for.

While Lieutenant Mundy was reading Carlos his rights, Dr. Afreen came running into the room, followed by Molly. She ran to her father and hugged him tightly.

"Is he okay? Did he hurt him?" asked Dr. Afreen, checking the machines around her patient and feeling for his pulse.

But before anyone could answer her, Carlos began laughing. He was laughing so hard that he could hardly breathe.

1 gambling [ˈɡæmbəlɪŋ] (a.) 賭博的
2 calmly [ˈkɑmlɪ] (adv.) 平靜地
3 reluctantly [rɪˈlʌktəntlɪ] (adv.) 不情願地
4 steadily [ˈstɛdəlɪ] (adv.) 穩定地
5 security officer 保全人員
6 burst through . . . 從……突然出現
7 securely [sɪˈkjʊrlɪ] (adv.) 牢固地
8 reinforcement [ˌriɪnˈforsmənt] (n.) 增援部隊
9 curse [kɜˑs] (v.) 詛咒

"Hurt him? Ha! Ha! Ha! Twice," he coughed, "I have tried to kill him twice . . . Ha! Ha! Ha!" He was laughing so hard he curled into a ball. "If I am cursed[9], then he is lucky! Ha! Ha! Ha!"

"Let's hope he finds jail just as funny," Lieutenant Mundy said.

Lucky

- Do you believe that some people are lucky? Discuss in small groups.

12

"My wife's name was Karis"

A week after Carlos had tried to kill Levy for the second time, Levy Andreas woke up. Dr. Afreen immediately called Haven police department. As soon as he heard that the old man was well enough to be interviewed[1], Molly's father called his daughter and together they went back to the hospital.

"I'd like to ask him a few questions. Is that okay?" said Molly's father.

They were on the sixth floor again and Dr. Afreen had met them outside Levy's room as soon as they had arrived.

"Sure," said Dr. Afreen. "He's just finished eating, so let's go in."

Inside, the old man was lying in bed. He turned his head toward them as they came in.

"Mr. Andreas, this is Lieutenant Mundy of Haven Harbor Police and this is his daughter, Molly," said Dr. Afreen. "They'd like to speak to you for a little while. Is that alright?"

The old man's eyes looked empty for a moment. Though his gray hair was neatly brushed, he looked very tired. His face was thin and his lips were dry.

Finally, he nodded his head. "Yes, yes. That's fine," he said, his voice not more than a whisper.

"Hello, Mr. Andreas," said Molly's father. "How are you?"

The old man smiled. "I'm still here," he said quietly.

Molly's father smiled, too. "Sir, what's the last thing you remember about *The Albatross*?"

"*The Albatross*?" said the old man. He swallowed².

Molly stepped forward and began pouring some water from the jug³ at the side of his bed into a glass.

"Do you remember *The Albatross*?" asked her father.

The old man shook his head very slightly. Molly gave him the glass, he drank and thanked Molly with a nod.

"I don't remember," said the old man. "I don't remember anything."

"Do you remember Carlos? The captain? Andre?" asked her father.

The old man shook his head.

"Don't worry, Mr. Andreas," said the doctor, replacing⁴ her chart. "Sometimes it can take a little while⁵ for your memory to return fully⁶."

Molly was looking at her father. He understood her unspoken⁷ question and he nodded.

---

1 interview [ˈɪntəˌvju] (v.) 面談
2 swallow [ˈswɑlo] (v.) 吞嚥
3 jug [dɪKg]
   (n.) 罐；壺

4 replace [rɪˈples] (v.) 放回（原處）
5 take a little while 花一點時間
6 fully [ˈfʊlɪ] (adv.) 完全地
7 unspoken [ʌnˈspokən] (a.)
   未說出的；心照不宣的

(57) Molly took the watch out of her pocket. Its hands were still stuck[1] at 1:38. She handed it to the old man, who took it hesitantly.

"To my darling Leveros 'Levy' Andreas," he said, reading the inscription and translating it into English. "All my love, K."

From outside, the sound of an approaching[2] ambulance filled the air. It grew closer and closer to the hospital until the siren[3] stopped suddenly, doors slammed and urgent voices called out.

Something else was happening. Molly could see that the old man's lip had begun to tremble[4]. Slowly, his face was changing, becoming less confused, less uncertain[5].

When he finally spoke, tears clouded[6] his eyes.

"Karis," he said. "My wife's name was Karis."

---

1 stick [stɪk] (v.) 卡住
（三態：stick; stuck; stuck）
2 approaching [əˋprotʃɪŋ] (a.) 接近的
3 siren [ˋsaɪrən] (n.) 警報器
4 tremble [ˋtrɛmbl̩] (v.) 顫抖
5 uncertain [ʌnˋsɝtn̩] (a.) 不確定的
6 cloud [klaʊd] (v.) 覆蓋

13

"Eventually, we feel grateful"

58

They were sitting in Levy's hospital room. Molly was on the chair and Levy on the bed with his legs swinging below him. They were waiting for one of the assistants[1] to bring a wheelchair[2] to take Levy to the hospital's front door. Finally, after nearly a month of treatment, today was Levy's last day in the hospital. He was happier than Molly had ever seen him.

"I'm fine. I can walk to the door," Levy had objected[3], but the head nurse[4] wasn't listening.

"Rules are rules," she said.

From outside the window, a beam[5] of sunlight fell into the room and lay across Levy's shoulders and chest. He was dressed in a new, dark blue shirt and a pair of jeans.

"Crazy," said Levy, smiling. "I'm fit[6] now. I don't need a wheelchair!" he said again.

Molly nodded. She had to admit the rule about wheelchairs did seem strange. Was this really the same man that she had seen on the beach just a few weeks ago?

"No running when we get outside, okay?" said Molly.

Levy laughed. "Yes, miss," he replied, his brown eyes twinkling[7].

---

1 assistant [əˈsɪstənt] (n.) 助手
2 wheelchair [ˈhwilˈtʃɛr] (n.) 輪椅

3 object [əbˈdʒɛkt] (v.) 反對
4 head nurse 護士長

They sat in silence for a few moments, each thinking their own thoughts. Molly knew she was going to miss him. She had visited Levy on all the twenty-six days he had been in the hospital, except one. When the soccer team bus broke down[8] two weeks ago on the journey back from a match[9] in upstate[10] New York, she had called him instead.

"Do you still miss her?" Levy asked suddenly.

They had talked about lots of things: Levy's home town of Nikiti and its view of the Aegean Sea[11]; Levy's house; Molly's father; her soccer team; her coach's[12] tactics[13]; and her friends. But it was Molly's mother and Levy's wife that they had discussed the least.

Molly didn't need to ask who "her" was. She nodded.

"How old were you?" he asked.

"Almost fourteen," Molly replied. "She died two days before my birthday."

"It's not easy: grief, I mean. At first, it is impossible. You understand?"

Molly nodded again.

"But slowly, the good things, the things that you loved about that person fill the emptiness[14]. Eventually, we feel . . ." he stopped, trying to search for the best word.

"Grateful[15]?" Molly offered.

---

5 beam [bim] (n.) 光束
6 fit [fɪt] (a.) 強健的
7 twinkle [ˈtwɪŋkl] (v.) 閃爍
8 break down 故障
9 match [mætʃ] (n.) 比賽
10 upstate [ˌʌpˈstet] (n.) 州的北部

11 Aegean Sea 愛琴海
12 coach [kotʃ] (n.) 教練
13 tactics [ˈtæktɪks] (n.)〔複〕戰略
14 emptiness [ˈɛmptɪnɪs] (n.) 空虛
15 grateful [ˈgretfəl] (a.) 感激的

"Yes. Grateful. That's exactly right, Molly. We feel it because we have known that person. You see, everything ends, Molly, but the trick[1] is to appreciate[2] the things we have when we have them."

"Did you always feel like that?" Molly asked. "I mean, grateful for Karis?"

Levy laughed. "It took me a long time to understand, too long. Some people understand it immediately. With others, it takes longer . . ."

Molly thought about her father. She wondered if he would ever feel the same as Levy did . . . as she did.

Grief

- Has someone important in your life died?
- How did you feel? Tell a friend.

"But listen," said Levy, his face breaking into[3] a smile again, "let's not be sad. We are here, we are healthy, and we have friends and family."

"Hello, you two!" said Dr. Afreen, coming into the room.

Levy turned around. "Doctor! Welcome. Molly and I were just chatting."

1 trick [trɪk] (n.) 詭計；把戲
2 appreciate [ə`priʃɪ,et] (v.) 感激
3 break into 突然開始（笑出來）

Dr. Afreen smiled. "Some things never change," she said and gave Molly a wink[1]. "You are going to wear your lungs out[2], Mr. Andreas."

Levy laughed. "Don't worry, Doctor. They are still strong."

Dr. Afreen smiled and signed the chart that lay hanging at the bottom of the bed.

"So, back to Greece?" she asked, pushing a strand[3] of her long, dark hair from her face.

"Yes, back home," replied Levy. "I have a brother in Nikiti, nieces and nephews, and a house that I want to buy. My brother and I have a little boat. We'll fish, we'll sell our catch[4] . . . You must come, Doctor, you and Molly."

Before Dr. Afreen could answer, the assistant came into the room, pushing a wheelchair.

"Ah," said Dr. Afreen, "your transport[5] has arrived."

Levy shook his head and sat down in it.

Dr. Afreen shook Levy's hand. "It's been a pleasure knowing you, Mr. Andreas. I wish you all the best[6]. Perhaps I'll make it to[7] Nikiti one of these days. Who knows?"

1 wink [wɪŋk] (n.) 眨眼
2 wear one's lungs out（話說太多而）感到疲倦
3 strand [strænd] (n.) 一縷（頭髮）
4 catch [kætʃ] (n.) 捕獲物
5 transport [trænsˋpɔrt] (n.) 交通運輸
6 all the best〔口〕祝一切順利
7 make it to 到達某地
8 square [skwɛr] (n.) 廣場
9 stand [stænd] (n.) 攤子；小販賣部
10 pickles [ˋpɪklz] (n.)〔複〕醃漬食品
11 mustard [ˋmʌstəd] (n.) 芥末
12 awesome [ˋɔsəm] (a.) 極好的
13 treat [trit] (n.) 款待；請（客）
14 eventually [ɪˋvɛntʃuəlɪ] (adv.) 最後地；終於地
15 cab [kæb] (n.) 計程車

"It's been a long time"

62 "So, what did you think of the show?" asked Molly's father.

They were standing in Times Square[8] in New York City, next to a hotdog stand[9]. Molly nodded and chewed for a second, her mouth full of hotdog, pickles[10], and mustard[11]. She swallowed.

"It was awesome[12]," she said. "Thanks, Dad. It was the best birthday present ever."

They had just been to see a show on Broadway. It was a surprise birthday treat[13] for Molly. Her father had given her the tickets that morning. What a way to celebrate her seventeenth birthday!

They walked up Broadway and toward Columbus Circle. They both noticed a Greek flag hanging up outside a restaurant. Molly stared as they went past. Her father looked, too. They said nothing, but each one remembered that day a year ago.

"You look tired," said her father eventually[14]. "You want to take a cab[15]?"

Molly nodded. They stopped and faced the oncoming[1] traffic.

"How's Levy?" asked her father, raising his arm and watching three yellow cabs rush past.

Levy had returned to the United States to be a witness[2] in the trial[3] of the captain and the crew of *The Albatross*. After the sentences[4] were passed[5] and the crew was put in prison[6], he had come to Haven and spent a few days there with them. Molly and he had continued to keep in contact with[7] emails and cards.

"He's good," replied Molly. "He and his brother have just bought a larger boat. They called it . . ."

"Molly?" asked her father, eyes on the traffic.

Molly smiled. "Karis," she said.

Just then, a yellow cab turned sharply and pulled up beside them.

"Riverside Drive, West 91st," said her father through the open window.

The cab driver nodded.

Molly and her father climbed in and the cab pulled quickly into[8] the traffic again. They were on their way to Molly's grandparents' apartment. For the first time since her mother had died, three years ago now, she and her father were going to stay with them.

---

1 oncoming [ˈɑnˌkʌmɪŋ] (a.) 迎面而來的
2 witness [ˈwɪtnɪs] (n.) 證人
3 trial [ˈtraɪəl] (n.) 審問
4 sentence [ˈsɛntəns] (n.) 判決
5 pass [pæs] (v.) 通過
6 be put in prison 被關進牢裡
7 keep in contact with 與……保持聯絡
8 pull into 駛進

Molly looked at her father's face. She decided that he looked tired; perhaps even a little tense.

She knew it was painful for her father going back to the grandparent's apartment[1], remembering her mother. But it was good to remember her and she never forgot Levy's advice: be grateful.

Molly took her father's hand and squeezed it.

Her father turned to her smiling. "What was that for?" he asked.

"Thanks," Molly simply said. "Thanks for everything, Dad."

The cab stopped and her father paid.

"Have a good evening, guys," said the taxi driver, smiling.

Outside, arm-in-arm[2], Molly and her father paused in front of the tall apartment block[3].

"It's been a long time . . ." said her father, looking up. Molly looked up, too.

On and on, shining out like stars, the lights from a thousand different rooms rose in front of them.

Her father took a deep breath. Molly smiled at him; and together, they stepped forward.

1 apartment [ə'pɑrtmənt] (n.) 公寓
2 arm-in-arm 臂挽著臂
3 block [blɑk] (n.) 街區

Ⓐ Personal Response

1 Read and answer the following questions on your own or with a partner.

ⓐ Did you enjoy the story? Which chapter did you enjoy the most?

ⓑ Which character was the most important in the story?

ⓒ Do you know someone who is as old as Levy? Describe him/her.

ⓓ Part of the story takes part on a big ship.

Have you ever traveled on one?

If you have, tell your classmates about it.

Where did you go?

Did you feel seasick?

Was it a long trip?

Would you go again?

ⓔ Discuss the role and importance of the different pets in the story: Herman and Pip.

ⓕ Do you think people should be allowed to have rare animals as pets?

ⓖ In your opinion, who deserves the longest prison sentence? (Choose between Carlos, Hopper, Andre or the captain.)

❸ Comprehension

2 Tick (✓) true (T) or false (F).

- ☐T ☐F [a] Levy was a cook on a ship called *The Albatross*.
- ☐T ☐F [b] After Levy finished the voyage, he planned to retire and live in the United States.
- ☐T ☐F [c] One night, Levy found rare birds called falcons in the ship's hold.
- ☐T ☐F [d] Levy didn't know that the captain planned to sell the falcons to a man called Hopper.
- ☐T ☐F [e] Levy fell into the ocean by accident.
- ☐T ☐F [f] Molly Mundy's dog found Levy lying on the beach.
- ☐T ☐F [g] Molly Mundy's father found a gold watch with an inscription on it.
- ☐T ☐F [h] Andre collected Levy's body from the beach and brought it to the ship again.
- ☐T ☐F [i] Molly Mundy's father inspected *The Albatross* when it arrived in Haven.

3 Correct the false sentences in Exercise **2**.

4 Did these events happen on the ship (S) or on land (L)? Check (✓).

S L ⓐ Lieutenant Mundy questioned the captain.

S L ⓑ The captain was arrested and handcuffed.

S L ⓒ Molly stopped the elevator.

S L ⓓ Lieutenant Mundy pointed a gun at Carlos for the second time.

S L ⓔ Andre was handcuffed by the police.

5 Why did these characters do these things?
Match the question with the correct answer.

_____ ⓐ At the start of the story, how did Levy know that Andre was in the hold?

_____ ⓑ Why did Levy go to see the captain?

_____ ⓒ Why did Levy not sink to the bottom of the ocean?

_____ ⓓ Why did Carlos dislike the captain?

_____ ⓔ Why did Pip suddenly look happy when he was outside the pet store and Molly was inside?

_____ ⓕ Why did Levy release all of the falcons?

_____ ⓖ Why did Carlos have a pillow in his hands when he was in Levy's hospital room?

_____ ⓗ Why did Carlos call Levy "lucky"?

1. He wanted to attract the police's attention to the ship.
2. He was tied with ropes and they weren't heavy enough.
3. He had survived many attempts to kill him.
4. He wanted him to call the police.
5. He wanted to use it to kill Levy.
6. He didn't trust him with the money.
7. He found an apple core belonging to him.
8. He saw Molly's father.

6 Can you remember these details from the story? Circle the correct answer.

a. Levy had spent nearly (50 / 55 / 60) years at sea.

b. Levy's gold watch was a present from his wife on his (40th / 50th / 60th) birthday.

c. The ship's cat was called (Harold / Herman / Henry).

d. There were nearly (30 / 40 / 50) cages in the hold.

e. When Molly woke up on Memorial Day Monday, the time was exactly (6 / 7 / 8) A.M.

f. When Molly found the gold watch, the time on it was (1:32 / 1:35 / 1:38).

C Characters

7 Match the brief descriptions below with the correct character. Write "M" for Molly, "L" for Levy, and "H" for Hopper.

Molly

Levy

Hopper

a _____ likes soccer.

b _____ has a dog named Pip.

c _____ is a store owner.

d _____ will soon retire.

e _____ is a criminal.

f _____ wants to buy a small boat.

g _____ was married to Karis.

h _____ is arrested.

i _____ is sixteen at the beginning of the story.

8 Who said it? Write Andre, Carlos, Molly, Hopper,
or Dan Mundy.

a *I don't like it. I just don't like it.
Murder wasn't part of the deal.*

b *I was just buying some dog food
. . . for my dog.*

c *I always knew you were a liar.*

d *He was dead! He was dead!*

e *I want road blocks on Highway
12 and CCTV footage of the area.*

f *If I am cursed, then he is lucky.*

Andre ☐   Carlos ☐

Molly ☐   Hopper ☐

Dan Mundy ☐

9 Complete the table with the correct names and adjectives.

the captain,
Carlos, Molly,
Levy, Andre

unintelligent,
greedy, resourceful,
violent, strong

Character		Adjective	Reason
Molly's father	is	smart	because he suspected the captain immediately.
a	is		because he fought with the captain and tried to kill Levy several times.
b	is		because he tried to cheat Carlos and Andre.
c	is		because he survived.
d	is		because he made several stupid mistakes.
e	is		because she used the Internet to find out more about the watch.

10 Work with a partner and discuss the following questions.

a Do you think Levy is a sociable person or not?

b Do you think Molly is a brave person or not?

96

D Plot and Theme

11 Put these sentences about the story in the correct order.

_____ a) Carlos held the bouquet of flowers tightly in his hand, trying to cover his face.

_____ b) Levy pulled the sheet away. He couldn't believe his eyes: a falcon!

_____ c) "You aren't going to like this," thought Andre and handed the binoculars to Carlos.

_____ d) "That's strange," thought Molly, watching the falcon as it flew over the beach.

_____ e) Slowly, with a pillow in his hand, Carlos moved toward the old man in the bed.

_____ f) With a mouth full of hotdog, pickles, and mustard, Molly smiled at her father.

_____ g) When the assistant brought the wheelchair, Levy didn't argue. He just sat down.

_____ h) Molly jumped across the pet store's counter and into her father's arms.

12 These three things are in the story. Say why they are important.

13 Why did it happen? Think about these events from the story and explain them to your partner. You may have to use your own ideas.

[a] Levy wanted the captain to call the police when he discovered the falcons.

[b] When Levy left the captain's cabin with the falcon, the captain called someone.

[c] Molly was unhappy when she woke up early on Monday morning.

[d] When Molly saw the falcon flying toward Haven, she was puzzled.

[e] Carlos and Andre probably threw Levy into the ocean at 1:38 A.M.

[f] At first, Molly didn't see Levy lying on the beach.

[g] Although Carlos told Andre to put chains around Levy's body, he didn't do it.

[h] When Molly, her father, and the police and medical services arrived on the beach, there was no dead body.

14 Complete these sentences with your own ideas and then discuss them with a partner.

a Molly couldn't understand the inscription on the gold watch that she found because _____

b At first, Molly's father thought that Molly made up a story about a body on the beach, but he changed his mind after he spoke to the captain because _____

c Carlos told Andre to bring Levy back to the ship when they saw his body on the beach because _____

d When Levy saw the gold watch in the hospital, he was upset but it actually helped him because _____

15 Think about the following questions and discuss them with your class.

a Who did Molly visit in the hospital when she was younger?

b Why did Levy call his boat *Karis*?

c Why did Levy and Molly talk about grief?

E Language

16 Complete the questions with the passive form of the verbs and then answer the questions.

ⓐ Who / Levy's watch / find by / ?

ⓑ When / the falcons / discover / ?

ⓒ Why / the falcons / smuggle / ?

ⓓ How many / times / Levy / nearly kill by Carlos / ?

ⓔ What / Carlos's face / cover by / in hospital corridor / ?

17 Read the sentences and report what the characters said.

What was the new engineer's name?

Leveros Andreas, but we called him Levy.

ⓐ

Has he said anything since he came in?

He's been unconscious the whole time.

b

18 Match the expressions from the story with their meanings.

_____ a) It was awesome.
_____ b) You gotta be kidding me!
c) I think we're done here.
_____ d) What's up?
_____ e) I haven't been there for you.

1) I can't believe what you are saying.
2) What's happening?
3) It was amazing.
4) I haven't been a good parent.
5) We have finished.

19 Put the words in color in order to complete the sentences.

a) If the police find the falcons, mean / it / will / us / for / trouble / all / of / .

b) If the police find Levy's body, the / spend / in / 20 / will / next / years / prison / we / .

c) If the pet store is closed, will / I / to / Marty's / go / .

d) If I am cursed, he / lucky / then / is / .

e) If I were you, would / and / I / pillow / drop / that / away / move / it / from / .

20 Complete the sentences using the correct verb form.

[a] The captain probably called Carlos and _____ (tell) him about Levy's discovery.

[b] Carlos and Andre _____ (fight) with Levy. Then Andre carried his body to the deck and _____ (throw) him overboard.

[c] At exactly seven o'clock in the morning, Molly _____ (wake) up, _____ (get) out of bed, and rubbed her eyes. She _____ (feel) terrible.

[d] Molly _____ (be) on the beach when she looked up and _____ (see) a falcon.

[e] Molly _____ (begin) walking toward Pip, who _____ (bark) loudly.

[f] When Molly reached the tree trunk, she _____ (find) the body that _____ (lie) behind it.

TEST

⭐ **1** Read and choose the correct answers.

_____ a Levy finds the falcons _____.

1 by chance

2 because he was searching for them

3 in the captain's cabin

4 deliberately

_____ b Andre and Carlos throw Levy overboard because Levy _____.

1 lose one of their falcons

2 discovers their secret

3 argues with the captain

4 slips and falls

_____ c When Molly returns to the beach with her father, he _____.

1 sees a falcon

2 doesn't want to speak to Molly

3 thinks Molly doesn't really see a body

4 is angry with Molly

_____ d Dan Mundy realizes Molly was tells the truth when _____.

    ① he learns that the ship is carrying TVs

    ② the captain tells him about Levy's accident

    ③ the captain becomes nervous

    ④ he speaks to Dr. Afreen

_____ e Carlos follows the captain to Hopper's store because _____.

    ① he wants his share of the $60,000 immediately

    ② he wants to see what Hooper looks like

    ③ he doesn't trust the captain

    ④ he wants to buy dog food

2 Listen to a news report about *The Albatross* and complete the form below.

Name of ship	*The Albatross*
Type of ship	**a**
People originally on the ship	**b**
	c
	d
	e
Time of arrival	**f**
Place of arrival	*Haven*
Registered cargo type	**g** *TVs*
Other cargo found on ship	**h**

3 Can you remember the words from the story to label the picture?

PROJECT WORK

Endangered birds

1 The Saker falcon is an example of an endangered bird. Use the words to complete the text below.

beautiful
birds
illegally
lives
number
nests

The Saker falcon usually _____ on open, grassy areas. It eats rats, mice, and other _____ such as pigeons. It often lives in old _____ that were made by other birds. It lays between 3–6 eggs. The _____ of Saker falcons is falling because it is losing its habitat and because more people are catching and selling it _____. There are probably less than 8,000 of these _____ birds still in the wild.

2 Use the Internet to find similar information about two other endangered birds. Find out which charities protect birds. Show your project to the class.

Birds as symbols

Web **3** Which countries have these birds as their national symbol? Do some research and find out.

peacock

golden eagle

emu

kiwi

gallic rooster

Saker falcon

4 If you could choose a bird to be the symbol of your classroom or your school, what would you choose? Make some suggestions and take a vote.

作者簡介

你們可以介紹一下自己嗎？

Scott 我正在攻讀教育博士學位，所以沒什麼時間從事休閒嗜好。不過，我很喜歡看小說，我目前正在讀 Patrick O'Brian 的小說。他寫了 21 本關於歐布瑞船長（Captain Aubrey）的《怒海爭鋒》系列小說，但我希望可以有更多本可以看。

Walter 我喜愛寫短篇小說，但我的工作很忙。我住在蘇格蘭，也在那裡工作，所以我常去山上健行。我的其他嗜好還有彈吉他和畫素描。

你們怎麼認識的？

Walter 我們讀小學的時候認識的，很多年以前了！

你們以前有一起合寫過小說嗎？

Scott 有，到目前為止，我們已經合寫過二十幾個故事了。

如何合寫一本書？

Walter 通常，我們其中一人有了想法後，我們會一起討論。因為史考特住在阿拉伯聯合大公國，而我在蘇格蘭，所以我們常在電腦上聊！

這本書有什麼寓意嗎？

Scott 我想，這本書有一部分是在講悲傷。當我們生命中重要的人去世時，我們得要記得那個人，但我們也要往前走。

這個故事的靈感來自何處？

Walter 史考特和我坐在海邊的一家咖啡館裡，那是個寒冷、下雨又刮風的夜晚。當我們從咖啡館的窗戶往外看時，我們看到一艘在克萊德灣的船所發出的光。我們納悶，那艘船載了什麼呢……

以後還會寫更多的故事嗎？

Scott **Walter** 那可多了！

1.「但那是不可能的」

P.13

信天翁號不是世界上最美的船,但雷夫洛‧安朱亞不在乎。他是這艘船的輪機員,大家都叫他雷夫。他今年六十五歲,有快五十年的時間都在海上度過,這是他最後一次出航。他等不及要退休,拿存款在他的家鄉希臘的尼基堤買一間房子。

他和另外兩名船員正載著電視機的貨物,朝黑文開去。這是他第一次搭信天翁號,但不是他第一次去黑文。多年前,當他太太還在世時,他曾和她一起造訪過這個位於美國東岸的小小港市。那是幸福的歲月。

雷夫看了看太太在他四十歲生日時送給他的金錶,「一點十四分!」他說。

他通常會盡量在十二點以前上床睡覺,但船上的貓,赫曼不見了。

P.14

有個暴風雨即將來襲,讓他很擔心。「等我找到那隻貓,我會宰了牠!」他一邊說道,一邊搖頭。

只剩下一個地方要找:貨艙。他開始爬下樓梯,來到最底層的甲板。就在他快走到樓梯底時,他停了下來。在他前方,貨艙的門半開著,裡面一片漆黑。按照慣例,那扇門因為安全理由,都是鎖上的。雷夫考慮立刻去報告船長,但接著他想到了赫曼。

雷夫在貨艙門口喊著:「赫──曼!

喂,赫──曼,你在裡面嗎?」

他拿出他的手電筒,「赫──曼!」雷夫又喊了一次。

手電筒只照亮了門口進去幾呎的地方,後方是一片黑暗,但雷夫很不想再走進去,事實是,他怕老鼠,而這也是他喜歡赫曼的一個原因。

雷夫站著不動。這時,船上下晃動的速度開始加快:暴風雨更加接近了。

「赫──曼──,你在哪裡?」雷夫大喊。

船長下令大家都不准進入貨艙,但雷夫得找到赫曼。雷夫遲疑地跨步往前走,但他的腳踩到了什麼東西。他往後跳開,往下看,一個蘋果核躺在他的腳邊。至少不是老鼠。

P. 15

「是安德烈！」雷夫心想。

安德烈老是把這些東西到處亂丟。他想像安德烈的臉，腦海中立刻浮現「大」和「蠢」兩個字。安德烈和同夥卡洛斯，是他的兩位同船的人員。雷夫盡可能離他們兩個遠一點，儘管這在一艘小船上並不容易辦到。

「我應該趕快離開這裡，那隻瘋貓會自己找路出來。我得去通報船長，說這扇門沒關好。」他想。

「啾咿──！」聲音從黑暗裡的某個地方傳來。

「啾──咿！啾──咿！」

聲音

▪ 你覺得發出這個聲音的是什麼？

「那是什麼聲音？」他喃喃自語說。

他將手電筒照進黑暗中，朝聲音走去。聲音再度響起，而且更大聲了。

P. 16

數百個盒子，高高地堆在他的身旁兩側，中間有一條空空的通道，就像峽谷中的一道河流。雷夫張大了嘴巴。在遠遠的貨艙那頭，從一扇半開著的門裡透出一束光來。

「不可能呀，貨艙裡沒有其他房間了。」他說。

但那裡有另一個房間，而且有另一道光，它吸引著雷夫往前走，猶如飛蛾撲火一樣。

2. 「我們遇到麻煩了」

P. 17

在房間外面，雷夫停下了腳步，他可以感覺到自己的心臟砰砰跳。他關掉他的手電筒，把頭伸進狹窄的門口。他第一眼看到的是一大張覆蓋著某個東西的床單。他走進房間，裡面到處都是床單。

他向前伸出一隻手，抓住最近的床單，把它拉了下來。

一隻雙眼閃閃發亮的美麗獵鷹，從籠子裡目不轉睛地回望著他。

「這到底是……？」他說道，並伸手去拉其他的床單。

在每張床單之下，出現更多的鳥兒。雷夫總共數了快四十個籠子，每個籠子裡面有一隻或兩隻的獵鷹。他勃然大怒，這些是特有種的鳥類，有法律保護牠們，以防像安德烈這樣的人。他想到了警察，「如果他們發現這些鳥，那我們所有人都會有麻煩了。我得去找船長。」

P.18

他拿起離他最近的一個籠子，走出貨艙，回頭爬上樓梯，來到船長室。他敲了敲門，然後直接走進去。

房間裡，船長坐在一張小書桌前，耳朵貼著手機。他偌大的身軀，讓房間看起來顯得更小。

「什麼事？」在雷夫走進來時，他厲聲問道。

「很抱歉打擾你，」雷夫回答道：「不過我在貨艙裡發現了這個。」接著，他舉起籠子。

船長瞪著獵鷹看。「我再打給你，」他對著手機說。

他的黑眼珠轉回雷夫身上。「你去貨艙做什麼？」他問。

「我去找赫曼，結果發現了這個，下面有四十幾個籠子。」雷夫回道。

接著是一陣沈默。「是安德烈，」雷夫繼續說道：「他要負責。」

「安德烈？你怎麼會覺得是他？」

「我發現一個蘋果……。」

「……那就表示是安德烈？」船長問道，臉上掛著一抹奇怪的微笑。

雷夫不解，因為這事可是非同小可的，他說：「船長，這些是稀有鳥類，我們大家可能因此去坐牢。」

船長似乎陷入沈思。

P.20

雷夫再度開口說道：「趁著警方還沒有進船查到這些鳥，我們打電話報警。」

船長緩緩點著頭，他回道：「當然，你說得對。」他繞過桌子，用手搭著雷夫的肩膀，「我會打電話報警，別擔心，一切都會沒事的，好嗎？」

雷夫點頭，說道：「好。」這才鬆了口氣，「我會把這隻鳥拿到我房間。」

船長點點頭，雷夫打開門，說：「謝謝，船長。」

一等到門關上，雷夫離開後，船長立刻用手機打給某個人。

「我們遇到麻煩了。」船長說。

雷夫沿著通往他的房間的走廊走著。他想把那隻獵鷹放在某個安全的地方。突然間，赫曼跑過去，尾巴豎得高高的。

雷夫大喊：「喂，你要去哪裡？」

赫曼沒有停下來，牠繼續全速奔跑，消失在走廊盡頭。

雷夫自己笑了起來，「真不敢相信！我以為，鳥應該要怕貓的才對。」

接著，雷夫聽到身後有聲音，他很快轉過身去，卡洛斯和安德烈就站在幾呎外，兩個人都冷冷地盯著他看。他們穿著連身工作服，看起來高大而粗壯。

P.21

「要去哪裡嗎？」卡洛斯問道。

「回我的房間。」雷夫回道。

卡洛斯笑了笑，他看著籠子，說道：「你拿了不屬於你的東西。」

雷夫感覺受到威脅。他太老了，打不過這兩個大傢伙。他想辦法要繞過他們。

「你知道現在幾點嗎？」安德烈突然問道。

雷夫看著手錶，差不多是半夜1點32分。突然，雷夫的頭部一陣尖銳的刺痛，眼前一切瞬間變為黑暗。當他睜開眼睛時，人已經躺在地板上，不過手中仍抓著那個籠子。

「老頭，你應該把獵鷹交給卡洛斯。」安德烈從卡洛斯的肩膀後方，語帶威脅地說。

卡洛斯把臉湊近雷夫的臉，對著雷夫說話，他的氣息充滿進了雷夫的鼻腔中。「老頭，別逼我揍你。」他低聲說道，綠色的雙眼閃爍著。

P.22

「船長……船長！」雷夫大喊道。

說時遲，那時快，卡洛斯一隻手掐著雷夫的喉嚨，另一隻手摀著他的嘴巴。

「笨老頭……」卡洛斯低聲說。

安德烈抓住籠子，想從雷夫的手中把籠子搶走。籠子向後摔了出去，撞到通往上層甲板的樓梯。籠子的門彈了開來。

「抓住牠！」卡洛斯大叫，伸出一隻手，但來不及了。

那隻獵鷹從他們上方打開的門飛了出去，消失在夜色中。下一刻，兩人轉身回到雷夫身邊。卡洛斯緊握雙拳。

安德烈敲了敲船長室的門。他身邊的卡洛斯，揉著自己的拳頭。

「進來。」

兩人走了進去。

「怎麼樣？」船長問道。

卡洛斯和安德烈彼此相覷。「我們出了點小問題。」卡洛斯說。

船長站起來，「我知道你們有麻煩！」

「雷夫讓那隻鳥飛走了。」安德烈謊稱。

船長一掌拍在桌子上，「那是一千元飛了！你們兩個白痴！」

安德烈看著地上，卡洛斯一雙眼閃爍著。

P. 23

「他人呢？」船長繼續説：「你們把他關在哪裡？」

「別擔心，我們已經把他料理好了。」卡洛斯答道。

「我們讓他洗了個澡，」安德烈像小孩一樣大笑：「有人落海啦！」

船長又坐了下來，看向小窗戶外面，映入眼簾的是黑色的天空。他們的計畫裡沒有那個老頭，現在他死了。這下好了！但是如果警方很快就發現他的屍體，他們就會有麻煩。警察會知道，那個老頭不是淹死的。

「別擔心，我們不會再見到他了。」卡洛斯説，看出船長的想法。

「希望是這樣，我當然希望是這樣。」船長説。

3. 「一隻獵鷹」

P. 24

16 歲的茉莉・蒙迪穿著一件長長的白襯衫，站在她的床邊，揉著眼睛。她的頭髮亂糟糟，感覺很不好。她半夜三點被暴風雨吵醒，過了好久都沒辦法再入睡。

當她看著她的鬧鐘時，發出了一聲呻吟。今天是星期一，是陣亡將士紀念日的星期一，而她在清晨七點整就完全清醒了。她轉身，看到正用興奮的眼睛看著她的皮普。

「我昨天晚上怎麼忘了關上房間的門呢？」她問自己。

皮普是她的狗，她很愛牠，除了牠跑進她的房間，用牠濕冷的鼻子貼在她臉上，把她吵醒。

她拉開窗簾，看向外面。天空很晴朗，幾乎沒有風。

「我想，我沒有藉口，嗯？」她問皮普。

看到牠猛搖尾巴，她很快套上牛仔褲，把她的黑色頭髮塞進紐約大都會隊的舊棒球帽裡。

P. 25

棒球帽

- 你知道紐約大都會隊是什麼嗎？上網做點研究，找出答案。
- 你覺得茉莉為什麼會有紐約大都會隊的帽子？
- 你有特別的帽子或 T 恤嗎？跟朋友分享。

「好了，我們走吧。」茉莉説。

皮普立刻來到她身邊，跟著她走下樓，進入起居屋。她穿上一雙白色的運動鞋，朝廚房喊著。

「我要帶皮普去貝殼灣。」她説。

「你吃過早餐了嗎？」她爸爸回喊道。

「嗯，不會去太久。」茉莉答道。

「嘿，你帶鑰匙了沒？我等下就要去上班了。」她爸爸説。

「有！」

「等你回來，要吃點早餐，好嗎？」

115

P.27

「好,再見。」茉莉回答道。在皮普擠過她身邊後,她走出門外。

貝殼灣在她家北邊,一片 C 字型的寬闊黃色沙灘,沿著海岸向北延伸三英哩到黑文。從她家要越過山丘,走十五分鐘路才會到海灘,但她很喜歡去那裡。從黑文來的其他人,有時候也會去那裡,但她猜這時候海灘應該沒人。

在山丘頂,茉莉轉身往回看。她爸爸對著她揮手,她也揮手回應。她看著他坐上車,離開去上班。很快,車子就看不見了,沿著十二號公路朝北往黑文而去。

她爸爸任職於黑文警隊,茉莉常常擔心他的安危,就像她母親以前那樣。

在她母親兩年前去世後,茉莉盡可能幫忙:列出購物清單、做家事、燙爸爸的襯衫,做這一類的事情。還有,遛皮普。

皮普迅速看了茉莉一眼,然後衝下山到海灘上。茉莉抓著她的帽子,也開始跑。不久,他們兩個就走在閃亮的海邊。

過了一會,茉莉撿起一根樹枝,正要丟出去時,她看見一隻鳥朝北方飛去。

P.29

「一隻獵鷹。」她悄聲說。

鳥從她頭上飛過去。她的雙眼跟著牠轉,直到牠變得太小,看不見為止。

接著,茉莉丟出樹枝給皮普撿。樹枝掉到靠近海邊的一株老樹幹的另一邊。皮普立刻追過去。當牠跑到樹幹時,牠跳過去,消失不見。

茉莉開始慢慢向牠走去,深深吸入早晨的清新空氣。一艘朝著黑文方向慢慢移動的船,吸引了她的目光。

「真高興我不在那船上。」她想,記起昨天晚上的暴風雨。

這時,皮普大聲吠了起來,她笑了笑,「牠找不到樹枝。」她想,開始找另一根。接著,她看見了沙子裡有個亮亮的東西。她伸手把它拿起來,那是一只手錶,一隻金錶,上面的時間是一點三十八分。她把手錶翻過來,錶背上有字,但她看不懂。「這是哪一國的字?」她心想。

皮普這時瘋狂地吠著。

「牠怎麼了?」她只能看到牠的尾巴在那根大樹幹後面。「什麼東西讓牠這麼激動?」

P. 30

這時，她可以看到牠的頭露在樹幹上面。牠四處跑來跑去，但眼睛盯著樹幹後面的什麼東西。

茉莉走得更近了……她站住，驚駭地瞪視。

一個老人躺在樹幹邊，臉朝天仰躺著。茉莉轉身，沿著海灘盡全力往回快跑。皮普跟在她後面。

茉莉
- 茉莉看見或發現了哪四樣東西是與故事的第一章有關？

4. 「有個東西，你得看一下」

P. 31

上午的陽光從船艙唯一的窗戶射入，黃色的太陽光照在船長寬闊的背部和他的黑色制服上。他的筆記型電腦打開著，放在他前面，他安靜地坐著，眼睛盯著螢幕看。安德烈和卡洛斯坐在他對面，注意看著他臉上的每一個變化。

這是暴風雨過後的上午，船平穩地航行在藍色的海面上。他們現在接近黑文了。再過幾個小時，他們就可以交出鳥，拿到他們的錢。

「昨天晚上的暴風雨好大，」安德烈說，並沒有特別對著誰講，「可惜，我們的輪機員沒有欣賞到！」

卡洛斯冷冷地看著安德烈。

安德烈笑了笑，露出一排黃牙，說道：「放輕鬆！「我知道故事是這樣：老頭生病了。他從船邊跌落海裡，我們盡力要救他，但手不夠長，抓不到他。然後，船長撥了求救電話給海岸防衛隊。」

「安靜，你們兩個！」船長說：「如果警方現在發現他，我們接下來二十年就要吃牢飯了，想想這一點！」他的話在空中迴盪了好一會兒。

P. 32

他關上筆電時，手機正好響起。他接起電話，立刻開始大吼。

安德烈傾身靠向卡洛斯，悄聲問：「是哈柏？」

卡洛斯點點頭。

「等等，」船長告訴打電話的人，一邊瞪著安德烈和卡洛斯：「去甲板上，注意警戒。」

安德烈和卡洛斯站起來，離開船艙。在他們身後，他們可以聽到和哈柏的通話持續著。安德烈一邊爬上往甲板的樓梯，一邊快樂地吹口哨。

然而，卡洛斯可一點也不快樂。他不喜歡船長和他說話的樣子，尤有甚者是，他不喜歡這筆買賣獵鷹的六萬元分配方式：船長怎麼會拿一半？為什麼他和安德烈才各拿到四分之一？走上甲板後，當安德烈把高倍雙筒望遠鏡推到他面前時，他還深陷在思緒中。

「有個東西，你得看一下。」他說，指著鄰近的一處海灘。

卡洛斯拿起望遠鏡，說道：「我不敢相信……」

P.33

「船長不會喜歡這種狀況的。」安德烈說。

卡洛斯那雙像綠色火焰的眼睛轉向他，「我叫你把他綁上鐵鍊，你有嗎？」

安德烈傻乎乎地看著卡洛斯，開始回答道，「有些舊的繩子……」

「你有沒有拿走他的身分證？」

安德烈沒有應聲，只見一抹驚慌的神色掠過他的臉。

「你這個白痴！」卡洛斯嘶聲說。

「我忘了！有太多事要做了，他很重，我沒辦法……」

「閉嘴！」卡洛斯大吼。

他得想一想，雷夫並沒有沈在他們下面深深的海底，而是像做日光浴那樣躺在海灘上。更糟糕的是，他的身分證還放在口袋裡。他知道，他得通知船長，坦承他的失誤：他是叫安德烈處理雷夫，而不是自己來。

但此刻，只有一件事要做：他們要把老頭的屍體搬離海灘，藏在船上的某個地方。

「上小艇，把老頭帶回船上，把他的屍體放到貨艙去。」卡洛斯說。

嘴巴張大的安德烈，站在那裡瞪著他看。

「上——小——艇，現在！」卡洛斯緩慢重覆了一遍。

5. 「對不起，爸」

P.34

有好幾個小時，警方都在海灘上來來回回地搜尋屍體，但什麼也沒找到。

茉莉看向越過山丘的小徑，警察一個

「我們可以去看場音樂劇，然後住在外公外婆家。」

茉莉也笑了。她爸爸在黑文出生，但她媽媽是紐約人，她外公、外婆還住在那裡，就是位在河濱路上的那棟房子，她母親就是在那裡出生的。她喜歡去紐約，尤其是百老匯。她想念那裡，也想念住在外公、外婆家。自從她母親去世後，她和爸爸就沒再去那裡住過。

不過，這次旅行的理由並不難猜，是拜今天之所賜。她猜想，爸爸覺得「海灘上的屍體」是一種想引起注意的呼喊，整件事都是她想像出來的。她不怪他。

她捏捏他的手。

「聽著，我得回辦公室去了，大概五點會回家，好嗎？」他輕聲說。

「嗯，好的。」茉莉點點頭說。

「你今天要練球嗎？」

P. 36

茉莉搖搖頭。黑文中學是地區的足球冠軍隊，而茉莉是女子隊的隊長。「那是昨天。」她說。

「昨天……」爸爸點著頭：「當然。」

「那只手錶呢？」茉莉問道。

「手錶？」

茉莉從牛仔褲的後褲袋裡掏出那只手錶。

爸爸瞄了手錶一眼。他的手放在她肩上，他們轉身，開始朝小徑入口走去。

「嗯，我想是有人掉了。」爸爸說：「你何不暫時先把它收起來，然後我們在馬提的商店櫥窗上貼個布告？」

茉莉在手上把錶翻過來，「上面刻的是俄文……或之類的。」她說。

接一個地，消失在山丘頂上。最後走掉的是兩名救護人員，抬著空空的擔架。

在她前面，盯著海看的是她的爸爸，爸爸穿著灰色港警的襯衫和褲子，站在海灘上。他戴的帽子，讓他看起來更加高瘦。

「對不起，爸。」茉莉終於開口，拉著他的手，抬頭往上看著他。

她不知道還能說什麼，那裡原先有具屍體的，她看到一名死掉的老人躺在沙灘上。但現在，那具屍體不在那裡，它消失了……說不通啊。

P. 35

他說：「這不是你的錯，我……我沒有待在你身邊，事實上並沒有。」他低下頭看著她：「你媽好去世之後，就沒有。」他的眼神變得溫柔而寬厚，「反正，我在想要休幾天假……去紐約。」他笑了笑，

不過，爸爸並沒注意，相反地，他正看著海上。等茉莉看到今天稍早那隻獵鷹時，爸爸還看著海面。現在，那隻鷹就在他們前方的山丘頂上。

「爸……」她說。但她一開口，那隻鷹就飛出視線外，不見了。

「嗯？」爸爸問道，轉身向她：「什麼事？」

「喔，沒什麼。」茉莉回答。

P.38

他們靜靜地走著，她的爸爸用手臂環著茉莉，把她拉近身邊。

「艾莉姑姑今天會過來嗎？」茉莉問道。

艾莉姑姑是爸爸的姊姊。爸爸不喜歡茉莉一個人在家裡，他說她年紀太小了。因此，艾莉姑姑通常在下午過來待幾個小時。

爸爸點點頭。

「可是，爸，我已經十六歲，不需要保姆了。」

爸爸笑了笑，「你還是我的小女兒。」

這句話讓茉莉想要尖叫，但她沒有，反而往前跑上山丘頂。

從遠方，在海浪聲與風聲之上，傳來獵鷹的叫聲。

茉莉一回到家，就上樓到她的房間，皮普緊跟在她後面。

在床上，她又讀了一次手錶背面的那個名字，「雷夫洛」。她又想到海灘上的那具屍體，不知怎地，她覺得這兩者有關連。她看著皮普，皮普對屍體的消失和手錶上的字一點興趣也沒有，牠躺在床腳，蜷起身體，眼睛已經開始闔了起來。她笑了笑。

P.39

艾莉姑姑要到下午晚一點才會來，而且茉莉不用上學或去練足球。她在吃早餐和在屋裡做些家事之前，有充分的時間可以做一點調查。

她打開筆電，把手錶背面的那些字，鍵入 Google 的翻譯機裡。過了一會，翻譯結果出來了。她慢慢複述那些字：「給我親愛的雷夫洛·『雷夫』·安朱亞。我全部的愛，K。」

這只手錶是某人送的禮物。那表示那位老人可能是某個人的祖父、某個人的叔叔，或者是某個人的丈夫。

資料

▪當你想要找資料時，你會去哪裡找或是做什麼？請打勾。
□百科全書
□圖書館
□網際網路
□報紙
□問大人或老師

6. 「他很緊張，問題是：為什麼？」

P.40

丹尼爾·蒙迪副中隊長剛剛花了兩小時，徒勞無功地在他家附近的海灘上尋找一具屍體。搜尋結束後，他回到辦公室，寫了一份報告。接著，他去警隊自助餐廳吃一份遲來的午餐。

他正喝著他那一天的第一杯咖啡時，他的上司走到他的桌邊說：「丹，一艘貨船剛剛進港了。」

蒙迪很想回答，「找別人去檢查」，但他沒有，那是他工作的一部分。

現在是下午兩點四十分，他正站在下層甲板，一手拿著文件，另一手拿著手電筒，執行例行性的貨物檢查。但有個聲音一直在他腦海裡，愈來愈大聲。這批貨和這個男人的舉止，有什麼地方不太對勁……

他轉向跟在一旁的男人，「你們載了多少電視？」他一邊問，一邊打開手電筒。

P.41

「什麼？」船長問。

船上引擎和發電機的噪音很大聲，講話要用喊的，不然很難聽得到。蒙迪副中隊長又問了一次，然後將手電筒的光照進貨艙的門裡。他用手電筒在房間四處照著，映入眼簾的是一個又一個的箱子。

「八百十五台。」船長回答，僵硬地站在門口。

蒙迪副中隊長緩緩地點著頭。

「就這些了。」船長補了一句。

「又來了：這個男人的聲音中……有什麼怪怪的。」蒙迪副中隊長心想。「了解。」他一邊說，一邊關掉手電筒。

蒙迪副中隊長走過信天翁號的船長身邊，「你確定，這是你所有的貨？」他一邊問，一邊從口袋裡拿出海關文件，眼睛一直盯著這個男人肥胖的臉。

「你整艘船都看過了。」船長回答。

「那並不表示我什麼都看到了，不是嗎？」蒙迪副中隊長問道，並笑了笑，可是船長沒有回應。

蒙迪副中隊長心想：「他很緊張，但問題是，為什麼？」

P. 42

他開始填寫文件，在「貨物」欄寫下「電視」，在「數量」欄寫下「815」。

「那麼，你會在黑文停留多久？」他問。

「幾天，大概兩天。」

蒙迪副中隊長點點頭。他仔細瞧了船長的臉，經驗是好老師。在黑文港警隊工作了二十年，丹·蒙迪遇過各式各樣的人。有時候，他們說謊的理由很蠢，但大部分的時候，人們會說謊是因為幹了非法的勾當。

P. 43

「船上有幾個船員？」他問。

船長像雕像一般靜止不動。「我自己和另外三個人。但你可能已經知道，輪機員很不幸失蹤了。」

蒙迪副中隊長瞪著那個男人，問道：「你說什麼？」

「我們有個人落海，我已經跟海岸防衛隊通報了。」

「什麼時候的事？」蒙迪副中隊長問。

「昨天晚上，大約凌晨三點時。」

蒙迪副中隊長那天早上到辦公室時，裡面靜悄悄的。今天是陣亡將士紀念日，來自其他機關，像是海岸防衛隊的報告，會比平常更晚才送到他桌上。即使如此，他還是很生氣：他應該更早知道這件事。

茉莉一再告訴他，她看見海灘上有具屍體的那個畫面，一直浮現在他的腦海裡。

「了解，很遺憾聽到這件事。你和他熟嗎？」

「不熟，可以說是不認識。我們原來的輪機員，剛好在啟航前生病了，所以……運氣真差，不是嗎？」船長回答。

「新的輪機員叫什麼？」

「嗯……雷夫洛·安朱亞，我們叫他雷夫。」船長回答：「他是個好人……真令人難過。」

P. 44

蒙迪副中隊長點點頭，「他是年輕人嗎？」

船長搖搖頭，「他是老人，希臘人。

我已經呈報詳情了。」

「是，想必是。」蒙迪副中隊長說：「那我想這裡一切都沒問題了，請簽一下這個。」

他把海關文件遞給船長。船長簽了名，還給他。

「祝你在黑文待得愉快。」蒙迪副中隊長說。

一抹隱約的微笑掠過船長的臉。

茉莉伸手拿起家裡的電話。

「嗨，寶貝，」茉莉的爸爸對著他的手機說：「在忙嗎？」

「沒有，只是在做晚餐。艾莉姑姑在這裡。」

「太好了！聽著，我打這通電話，是因為我想為稍早的事情道歉……我不知道是怎麼回事，但我想你是對的。」

「你是說什麼事？」茉莉問。

「我想，你的確在海灘上看到某個人。事實上，我很確定是這樣。我只是想說，我很抱歉……」

「沒關係，事情有點怪。」茉莉打斷他：「我是說，前一分鐘，海灘上還有屍體，下一分鐘就不見了。」

P.45

「是啊。無論如何，我只想說對不起，好嗎？」

「好。」茉莉回答。

「對了，你說，你看到的那個人年紀很大了？」

「對，可能快七十了。我是說，以他的白頭髮和……」茉莉回道。

「好，我想知道的就是這些。晚點見……」爸爸正準備掛斷電話，但茉莉阻止了他。

「爸，等一下，你想，那只手錶是不是他的？」她說。

「什麼手錶？」他問。

「我今天早上在海灘上發現的錶，你知道的，就是背面有刻字的那個錶。我知道那些字的意思了，那是希臘文，手錶的主人是某個叫安朱亞的人……」

123

7. 「我們帶鳥來，他帶現金來」

P.46

那三個人圍坐在船上廚房的一張桌子邊，港警才走了十分鐘，但信天翁號的船長已經忘了副中隊長的名字。

當卡洛斯問他事情的經過時，船長聳聳肩，說道：「條子問了些問題，沒什麼好擔心。」

「那現在怎麼辦？」卡洛斯問。

船長說：「哈柏要我晚點去鎮上跟他碰面。交易安排在清晨四點。我們帶鳥，他帶現金。」

哈柏是他們走私動物的買主，而且他只想和船長交易。這讓卡洛斯很火大。

為什麼船長可以拿三萬元？他的工作有加倍危險嗎？他有加倍聰明嗎？

卡洛斯心想，「一定有什麼方法可以讓哈柏信任我，我要拿到哈柏的電話號碼，或者……」，另一個計畫逐漸在他的腦中成形。

P.48

安德烈吃完蘋果，用袖子擦擦嘴巴。「警察呢？」他問，眼睛從船長的臉轉向卡洛斯的臉。

「怎樣？」船長問。

「他們會再回來嗎？」

「有可能。我給他們看了貨物和我們的護照，但他們會想要查核我們對於雷夫的說詞。」船長回答，站起身來。

「你為什麼要一個人去見哈柏？」卡洛斯突然問。

船長一聽，吃驚了好一會兒，一句話都說不出來，頓時一陣沈默。接著，他吐出一大口氣，冷冷地笑道：「很簡單，哈柏是個很神經兮兮的人，而你們，我的朋友，你們會讓他更緊張。」

雖然是向晚時分了，太陽仍明亮地照耀著，而且很熱。不過，茉莉正步行於樹下，享受著樹蔭下的涼爽、松樹的強烈氣味，還有皮普追著鳥兒跑的畫面。

P.49

她走在繞過山丘前往黑文的狹窄小徑上。稍早之前，艾莉姑姑注意到，他們家的狗食快沒了。

「我去買，我得去走走。」茉莉立刻說。

在群木中最高的那棵樹下，她看了看手錶，快四點半了。

她想：「希望寵物店還開著，畢竟，今天是陣亡將士紀念日。如果打烊了，我就去馬提的店，」茉莉想：「至少，我可以在那裡買到一些肉罐頭。」

馬提的店是當地的藥房雜貨店，從來不休息。

皮普這時走在她身邊，過了一會，他們兩個走出樹林，步上黑文的大街。

「別擔心，我們就快到了。」她告訴皮普。

她伸出手要給皮普繫上狗鍊，但牠猛然把頭轉開，跑去追在附近一道矮牆上的兩隻海鷗。海鷗看著牠大聲喧鬧地跑過來後，伸出長長的翅膀，懶洋洋地從牆上飛起來，然後越過屋頂。

皮普和茉莉看著牠們朝樹林飛去，接著突然改變方向，俯衝而下，反而朝著開闊的海洋飛去。

P. 50

茉莉感到不解，她瞧了瞧，看看是怎麼一回事。從太陽的方向，飛來了一個黑色的物體。她瞇起眼睛看，那是一隻獵鷹，搞不好就是海灘上那一隻。獵鷹從頭上快速低空飛過，然後停在一座倉庫的屋頂上，就在碼頭一艘的船旁邊。

皮普叫著。

「我們去幫你買些食物吧。」她說。

一會兒後，他們來到寵物店外面。茉莉把皮普綁在欄杆上，走了進去。

在寵物店對面的一棟房子裡，伯格森小隊長從窗簾前面退開，轉身向著蒙迪副中隊長。

「長官，你得看一下這個。」

「是什麼？」蒙迪副中隊長問，一邊走向窗邊。

他拿過望遠鏡，一瞬間，停止了呼吸。

「我們該怎麼辦，長官？」

「通知這裡的霹靂小組！現在！」丹．蒙迪大吼道。

警察
- 用望眼鏡在觀察的警察是誰？
- 什麼是霹靂小組？他們的工作是什麼？上網找出答案。

8. 「謀殺不是交易的一部分」

P. 51

店裡面，乾草和小動物的慣有氣味，傳入茉莉鼻中，但櫃台後面沒有人。她從架子上拿了兩罐狗食，心想，「我應該只要把錢放在收銀機旁邊嗎？」

這時，她聽到聲音，是從店的後方傳

出來的。她手裡仍拿著罐頭，一邊走到櫃台後面。一扇通往另一個房間的門，開了一條小縫。

「一切都沒問題，」一個男人的聲音從門後面傳來，「我們遇到了一點小麻煩，但一切都沒問題。」

「麻煩？」另一個人問道。

茉莉認得那個聲音，那是寵物店老闆哈柏先生。

「我們得把他帶回船上。一等我們開到深水區，我們會再把他的屍體丟下去……」

「我不喜歡這樣，就是不喜歡。謀殺不是交易的一部分……」哈柏先生回道。

P. 52

「閉嘴！不需要你喜歡。雷夫由我來操心，你操心要付給我的那八萬元吧。」

茉莉幾乎喘不過氣來。她得離開這裡，去告訴她爸爸，說明她剛聽到的事。她轉過身來。

一雙綠色的眼睛直直瞪著她看。

「小女孩有大耳朵，」站在她面前的男人說：「可能聽到了不該聽的事情。」

有那麼一秒鐘，茉莉考慮衝過這個男人，但他偌大的身軀，完全堵住了她和前門之間的空間。她往後退了一步。

那個男人沒有動作，也沒有吭聲，但茉莉很害怕。是他的眼睛，他那雙綠色的小眼睛，像鋼鐵一樣又硬又無情。

茉莉感到心臟開始加速跳動。透過窗戶，她可以看到皮普在外面的欄杆旁邊。牠站著，注意看著那個男人的一舉一動。牠露出了牙齒，耳朵平貼在頭上。

「我只是來買一些狗食……給我的狗。」茉莉說道，努力要維持呼吸平穩，努力要聽起來很勇敢。她舉起那兩個罐頭。

那個男人沒說話，但他那雙綠色的眼睛繼續瞪著她。

P. 53

「想想辦法！」茉莉腦袋裡的某個部分大喊道。

她看看四周，在她後面，在短短的走廊尾端，她看到另一扇門。那是出口？還是儲藏室？

有著綠色眼睛的男人，似乎察覺到她的想法。在茉莉移動之前，他的手臂舉起來靠著牆壁，擋住了她的路。

「放輕鬆。」他說，氣息噴到她臉上。

險境

■ 你曾身處險境嗎？跟朋友分享。

「誰在那裡？」一個聲音喊道。

茉莉轉身，那扇半開的門，猛然打開。一個穿著黑色褲子和黑色外套的大塊頭男人走向前，後面跟著臉色蒼白的哈柏先生。

「你在這裡做什麼？」穿著黑色制服的男人大叫。

P. 55

綠眼男子笑了起來，「跟蹤你。」他鎮定地說。

「怎麼回事？」哈柏先生問。茉莉和他兩個人，現在都站在櫃台後面。「他是誰？還有，她在這裡做什麼？」他問，豎

起姆指用力指著茉莉。

那兩個男人不理他。相反地,他們隔著幾呎,面對面站著。從櫃台後面,茉莉可以清楚看到皮普。牠大聲吠叫,扯著錬子,想掙脫項圈。

「他叫卡洛斯,而且,他正要走了。」穿黑色制服的男人說。

卡洛斯又笑了起來。「我想不是這樣,船長和我有事情要談。」他說。

「我們沒有什麼要談。」船長回答。

「你錯了。你看,我想要你解釋一下,六萬元和八萬元的差別。」卡洛斯鎮定地說。

「他在說什麼?」哈柏問,傾身橫過櫃台朝向兩人。

在外面,茉莉看到皮普已經不再使勁想掙脫了。相反地,牠靜靜地站著,尾巴快樂地搖擺著。「好奇怪。」她想。

「他在胡說。」船長說。

P. 56

卡洛斯臉色變了,「我一直都知道你是個騙子。」他說。

突然間,卡洛斯朝船長衝過去,手裡拿著刀。船長及時舉起手臂,擋住卡洛斯刺向他胸口的一刀。船長抓住卡洛斯的手腕,兩個人打了起來,撞倒架子和籠子。

茉莉從眼角看到店外面有件灰色制服……接著,一切瞬間發生。卡洛斯揮刀朝船長的脖子刺去;哈柏尖叫;店後方的門被撞開;空中充滿喊叫聲;哈柏舉起雙手;警察把兩個男人壓在地上;茉莉跳過櫃台,撲進爸爸的懷裡。剎那間,一切就結束了。

茉莉安全地在店外面,肩膀上披著條毯子,看著卡洛斯、船長和哈柏被銬上手銬,分別上了三輛警車。

爸爸用手抱著她,給了她一個大大的擁抱。

「我沒事,爸,真的,我沒事。」她說,一邊阻止皮普跳上來,舔她的臉。

爸爸注意到她的手在發抖,這是受到驚嚇的典型症狀。「讓他們給你檢查一下,好嗎?就當為了我。只要兩分鐘,我保證。」

P. 57

茉莉太累了,沒力氣爭辯。「好。」她說,然後把皮普的錬子交給爸爸,「你贏了。」

爸爸笑了笑。當她轉頭看時,他們已經快走到救護車了。

載著卡洛斯、哈柏和船長的警車,

慢慢沿著大街開，但群眾並沒有看著他們。相反地，大家都在看著其他的東西，在天空的什麼東西。她停下腳步，也抬頭往上看。

天空中都是獵鷹。牠們似乎都是從港口裡的一艘船來的，而且立刻向四面八方飛去。

9. 「他死了！」

P. 59

在救護車後面，茉莉坐在床沿，救護人員在幫她量脈搏。從打開的車門，她看到愈來愈多獵鷹飛上天空。

「這真是太奇怪了，」茉莉對爸爸說：

「你想，牠們是從哪裡來的？」

「我不確定。」他回答，遮著他的眼睛擋太陽，「但我覺得和我稍早前去過的那艘船有關係：信天翁號。」

「你呼吸有困難嗎？」救護員問茉莉。

她搖搖頭。

爸爸拿出手機，按了一個號碼。「嗨，艾莉，是我。」他說。茉莉可以隱約聽到姑姑回應的聲音。爸爸開始解釋事情發生的經過。茉莉可以想像姑姑的表情。

「不，她沒事……」爸爸說：「她沒事……她沒事。」

P. 60

茉莉笑起來。

爸爸電話聽了一會，說道：「是的，好。」

過了一會兒，講完電話後，他收起電話，轉身向著茉莉，說道：「你艾莉姑姑要過來。」

茉莉點點頭。

幫茉莉做檢查的救護員告訴爸爸，說道：「她受到嚴重驚嚇，但她的血壓、呼吸和脈搏都正常。」

「我就說了嘛！」茉莉說。

「很好，因為等艾莉姑姑來了，我要你和她一起回家去。我要到碼頭去。」爸爸說。

「可是，爸，那不公平。」茉莉大叫。

爸爸笑了笑，「你一天的刺激量夠多了。」

蒙迪副中隊長站在信天翁號旁邊的碼頭上，手裡拿著大聲公，舉起左手。他正向他的手下打信號，叫他們等一等。

像這樣的狀況，都會讓他很緊張，因為諸多情況不明。第三名船員會輕易投降嗎？他有槍嗎？船上還有其他人嗎？只有一個辦法可以知道，那就是他們要登船。

「我是黑文警隊副中隊長蒙迪，出來，我們已經包圍了這艘船。」他說。

P.61

他的聲音透過喇叭轟轟作響，在船隻的鋼製船身裡發出回聲。他等著，沒有回應。他轉身，揮手叫手下前進。立刻有六名警官越過他，開始沿著窄窄的跳板跑上船，手裡拿著槍。他們幾乎一踏上船，就開始大喊。

「出來！」他們大吼：「跪下，跪下！」

慢慢地，有一雙手，然後是一顆頭出現在通往下層甲板的一個樓梯間。最後，一名高大的男子現身，雙手高舉在空中。那是安德烈，他臉色發白，兩眼直視。

「不！」安德烈大叫：「他死了。他死了！」

瞬間，港警包圍了他。他們把安德烈壓在地上，戴上手銬，但那個男人還是繼續說。

「我看到他，我看到他，我看到他了。」他呻吟著。

猜猜看

■ 安德烈說的是誰？

P.63

「蒙迪副中隊長！」伯格森小隊長喊著，他在安德烈上來的那道樓梯底部，「你得來看一下這個。」

蒙迪副中隊長很快走下樓梯，到了底層甲板。伯格森小隊長和另兩名警官站在通往貨艙那扇門前面。雖然，裡面的電燈打開了，還是幾乎一片黑暗。蒙迪副中隊長打開他的手電筒，走進門口。

這一次，場景非常不一樣。這一次，箱子不再排列整齊。

「看起來有場打鬥。」他想。

但這還不是最大的不同之處。在貨艙的那一邊，在地板上亂七八糟堆著的箱子再過去，有一扇半開的門，透出一道明亮的光線。現在，一切都說得通了。這個貨艙比一般貨艙小，他是對的。原因很簡單，有一道假牆把貨艙隔成兩部分。

他掏出槍，無聲地打信號，叫他的一個手下往左，另一個往右。他、伯格森小隊長和其他人，則慢慢往前走。

隨著愈走愈近，他們可以看出來，那道假牆有多像貨艙真正的牆壁。那牆是用薄木板做成，但漆上和真正貨艙一模一樣的顏色。事實上，如果不是門打開，沒有人會知道那裡有個祕室。

P.64

他們四個人全走到那道假牆前，背靠著牆，排成一列。蒙迪副中隊長右手持槍，用左手的手指開始倒數，……三……二……一。

蒙迪副中隊長在前，後面跟著伯格森

小隊長，然後是另兩名警官，他們衝進門去，身體緊繃，槍拿好準備著。

那裡，在那個小房間裡，在一堆空空的鳥籠中間，躺著一個老人，他的臉向著另一邊，他的衣服潮濕，白髮緊貼著頭皮。

蒙迪副中隊長跪下來，伸手摸老人的手腕。他把手指壓著血管，老人的皮膚冰冷。蒙迪副中隊長開始鬆開手指，準備放下老人的手腕。但接著，他感覺到了最輕微的脈搏。

「叫救護車，」他大喊：「他還活著。」

老人
- 你記得發生在這老人身上的所有事情嗎？回頭看故事，找出來。

10. 「鞋子！」

P. 65

茉莉第一次來黑文醫院是在她九歲那年，那時她從腳踏車上摔下來，跌了個狗吃屎。她的下巴割傷，血流到她的新 T 恤上。等她回到家，她媽媽從浴室拿了一條黃色的毛巾幫她包起來，然後很冷靜地開車載茉莉去黑文醫院。她還記得，媽媽溫暖的手抱著她；黃色毛巾變成紅色；醫院的門打開，那個氣味第一次迎向她。

她第二次去醫院時，同樣的氣味迎接著她。這一次，她媽媽正在接受癌症治療。茉莉盡可能把氣憋得久一點，這是個無聊的遊戲。一個月之後，當她媽媽去世時，茉莉憋了兩分鐘。

今天，她又再次來到醫院，被她所痛恨的同樣熟悉而刺鼻的氣味所包圍。

P. 66

她在一台往上到六樓的電梯裡，一名拿著病歷資料的護士站在她前面，面對著電梯門。她旁邊是穿著灰色制服的爸爸，身上配著槍。這一次，她和爸爸是為了警方公務而來。這一次，茉莉沒有憋氣。

氣味
- 你可以想出一個有特殊氣味的地方嗎？告訴朋友。

電梯門打開，一名有著深色長髮的高大女子走向前來自我介紹。「我是艾芙

琳醫師。我想，你們是來看安朱亞先生的。」她說，對茉莉笑了笑。

「沒錯。」茉莉的爸爸回道。

他們開始沿著走廊走去。

「他入院後，有說過什麼話嗎？」

「他一直在昏迷。」艾芙琳醫師答道。

P. 68

茉莉的爸爸點點頭，「沒關係。我們從船上的其中一人那裡，知道了一些他的事。聽起來，安朱亞先生是船上的輪機員。他發現船上的同事走私罕見鳥類，威脅要報警。」

醫師搖搖頭，「所以，他們決定殺掉他？」

「是的，」茉莉的爸爸回答道：「他們把

他丟下海，但他出現在海灘上。就在這時，我女兒茉莉看到他……」

「你一定覺得很可怕。」醫師說，閃亮的淡褐色眼睛看著茉莉。

「他們把他帶回船上，關在貨艙裡。他們在等到達深水區時，要把他再度丟到海裡去……」茉莉的爸爸繼續說。

「太壞了。」醫師低聲說。

「我只是要茉莉正式指認他，確定他就是她在海灘上看到的人，可以嗎？」

「當然。」艾芙琳醫師說。她打開門，領他們進了病房。

「是他。」茉莉看到躺在床上的老人後，低聲說道。

「你百分之百確定，他就是你在海灘上看到的老人？」爸爸問道。

茉莉點點頭。

P. 69

「好。」茉莉的爸爸說著，一手抱著她，「我想，這樣就可以了，謝謝你抽空。」

「不客氣。」艾芙琳醫師說。她關上門，再度和茉莉以及她爸爸走出來到走廊上。

「等安朱亞先生醒來後，我再過來。」茉莉的爸爸說，但當艾芙琳醫師要開口回答時，響起了廣播聲：「艾芙琳醫師，請到六十七號病房。艾芙琳醫師，請到六十七號病房。」

她聳聳肩，說道：「抱歉，我得走了。」她開始快速走下走廊，「很高興認識你們。」她說。

茉莉和爸爸看著她離去。

「她人很好，你不覺得嗎？」茉莉說。

爸爸笑了笑，但沒説話。他們開始再次朝著電梯走去。茉莉注意到，走廊上醫院的味道，甚至比在病房裡還強烈。就在這時，爸爸的手機響了。

「哈囉？」爸爸説。他暫時沒説話，注意聽著電話另一端的聲音，「你一定是在開我玩笑吧！」他突然説，幾乎是用喊的，「別管事情怎麼發生了，我們晚點再來想。現在，我們得集中人力找到他……」

P. 70

他在説什麼？發生什麼事了？

「……我要在十二號公路設路障，還有我要那個地區的監視器畫面……」爸爸繼續説。

茉莉注意到有個男人，沿著走廊朝他們走來。他拿著一大束花，大到把他大部分的臉擋住了。她並沒有太注意看他，但她剛好瞄到他的腳。她看到的景象，讓她有點困惑。

爸爸講完電話，他們繼續朝電梯走去。「真不敢相信。」爸爸生氣地説。

「怎麼了？」茉莉在電梯來時問道。

爸爸吐出一大口怒氣，「是卡洛斯，他被放出警察局了。」他説，看著電梯門打開。

「卡洛斯？可是，怎麼會？」茉莉問。

他們走進電梯。

「行政疏失。他被誤認為別人，然後被誤放……」爸爸回答道，按下「G」字的按鈕。「他在監獄裡，」他繼續説：「然後，他剛剛走出去了……」

電梯門開始關上，在逐漸關上的門中間，走廊變得愈來愈窄，愈來愈窄……

P. 71

突然，茉莉把她的手臂，像劍一樣筆直地插入即將關上的門中間。有一秒鐘，茉莉的手被夾得很痛，她叫了出來。然後，門往反方向打開，再度看到整個走廊。

「鞋子！」茉莉説，揉著她的手臂，走出電梯，「那個男人，那個拿著一大束花，在走廊經過我們的人——他的鞋子沒有鞋帶……」

爸爸看著她，好像她的話沒有意義。

「跟監獄裡的一樣，跟監獄裡的一樣！」她説。

11. 「如果我被詛咒，那算他好運」

P. 72

「如果我是你，我不會那麼做，」蒙迪副中隊長説。

兩隻熾熱的綠色眼珠轉過來，瞪著現在直直對著他們的槍。

「丟掉，」蒙迪副中隊長沈著嗓子説：「現在！」

卡洛斯慢慢地把枕頭從老人的臉上拿開，等枕頭移到床外，他鬆開手。枕頭從他手中落下，發出輕微的砰一聲，落在已經掉在地上的花束旁邊。

「從他身邊退開，輕輕慢慢地。」

卡洛斯的眼睛仍盯著槍，從雷夫躺著的病床邊退開幾呎。他一邊退開，一邊瞄向病床另一邊牆上的窗戶。

蒙迪副中隊長笑起來，說道：「我不會阻止你，不過我要提醒你，我們在六樓高。現在，跪下，手放在頭上。現在！」

卡洛斯的身體變得像彈簧一樣緊繃，蒙迪副中隊長可以察覺他的想法。這個有著狼一般綠色眼睛的男人，正在計算攻擊他並奪走槍的機率。

P.74

「如果你是賭徒，那麼儘管放手一試⋯⋯」蒙迪副中隊長冷靜地說。

卡洛斯不情願地先跪下一隻膝蓋，再跪下另一隻。他舉起雙手，放在頭頂。

「雙腳在背後交叉，快點照做！」蒙迪副中隊長命令。

蒙迪副中隊長的槍穩穩地指著卡洛斯，伸手去拿一向掛在腰帶上的手銬。

就在這時，三名醫院的警衛從他身後的門衝進來。不一會兒，卡洛斯就被牢牢地銬上手銬，趴在地上。三名警衛站著監視他，等著蒙迪副隊呼叫的增援警力到來。

當蒙迪副中隊長在宣讀卡洛斯的權利時，艾芙琳醫師跑進房間，茉莉跟在後面。她跑向爸爸，緊緊抱著他。

「他沒事吧？他有沒有傷到他？」艾芙琳醫師問，一邊檢查在她病人身邊的機器，一邊量他的脈搏。

但在有人回答她之前，卡洛斯開始大笑。他笑得很猛，都快喘不過氣來了。

「傷到他？哈！哈！哈！」他咳著：「兩次，我兩次想殺死他，哈！哈！哈！」他笑得很用力，身體蜷成一團，「如果我被詛咒了，那算他好運！哈！哈！哈！」

「希望他覺得監獄也一樣好笑。」蒙迪副中隊長說。

好運

- 你相信有些人就是好運嗎？小組討論。

12. 「我太太叫凱莉絲」

P.76

在卡洛斯企圖第二次殺害雷夫之後一個星期，雷夫·安朱亞醒了。艾芙琳醫師立刻打電話給黑文警察局。茉莉的爸爸一聽說老人已復原到可以接受訊問，立刻打電話給女兒，然後一起回到醫院。

「我想要問他幾個問題，可以嗎？」茉莉的爸爸問。

他們又來到六樓，艾芙琳醫師在他們一抵達後，就在雷夫的病房外等他們。

「當然可以，他才剛吃過飯，我們進去吧。」艾芙琳醫師説。

病房裡，老人躺在床上。在他們進來時，他轉頭看他們。

「安朱亞先生，這位是黑文警隊的蒙迪副中隊長，這位是他的女兒茉莉，他們想要和你談一下，可以嗎？」艾芙琳醫師説。

有好一會兒，老人眼神空洞地看著。雖然他的白髮梳得很整齊，但他看起來非常疲倦。他的臉頰消瘦，雙唇乾燥。

P. 77

最後，他終於點點頭，説道：「好，好，沒關係。」他的聲音氣弱游絲。

「哈囉，安朱亞先生，你好嗎？」茉莉的爸爸説。

老人露出微笑，「我還在這裡。」他低聲説。

茉莉的爸爸也露出微笑，「先生，關於信天翁號，你記得的最後一件事是什麼？」

「信天翁號？」老人説。他吞了吞口水。

茉莉走向前，拿起在他床邊的水壺，開始把一些水倒進玻璃杯裡。

「你記得信天翁號嗎？」爸爸問道。

老人微微地搖了搖頭。茉莉把玻璃杯遞給他，他喝了水，對茉莉點頭致謝。

「我不記得了，我什麼都不記得了。」老人説。

「你記得卡洛斯嗎？船長？安德烈？」爸爸問。

老人搖頭。

「別擔心，安朱亞先生。」醫師説，把病歷表放回去，「有時候，要過一陣子，你的記憶才會完全恢復。」

茉莉看著爸爸，他了解她沒説出口的問題，於是他點點頭。

P. 79

茉莉從口袋裡拿出手錶，錶的指針還指著一點三十八分。她把手錶拿給老人，他遲疑地接過去。

「給我親愛的雷夫洛．『雷夫』．安朱亞，」他唸著上面刻的字，並把它翻譯成英文，「我全部的愛，K。」

外面，救護車接近的聲音響徹雲霄。它愈來愈接近醫院，直到警笛聲突然停止，門猛然打開，急迫的聲音叫嚷著。

有其他什麼事發生了。茉莉可以看到老人的嘴唇開始顫抖。慢慢地，他的表情改變了，變得沒那麼困惑、迷惘。

當他終於開口説話時，他的雙眼充滿淚水。

「凱莉絲，」他説：「我太太叫凱莉絲。」

13. 「最終，我們會覺得感激」

P. 80

他們坐在雷夫的病房裡。茉莉坐在椅子上，雷夫坐在床沿，雙腳在身下搖晃。他們在等一個病房助理員推輪椅過來，好把雷夫送到醫院大門口去。終於，在經過約一個月的治療後，今天是雷夫在醫院的最後一天。茉莉沒看他這麼高興過。

「我很好，我可以走到門口去。」雷夫抗議，但護理長不理他。

「規定就是規定。」她説。

一束陽光從窗外照進房裡，照在雷夫的肩膀和胸口上。他穿著一件新的深藍色襯衫和一條牛仔褲。

「瘋了，」雷夫笑著説道：「我現在很健康。我不需要輪椅。」他又説了一次。

茉莉點點頭，她得承認，關於輪椅的規定聽起來的確很奇怪。這真的是她不過幾星期前，在海灘上看到的同一個人嗎？

「等我們到了外面，不要跑，好嗎？」茉莉説。

雷夫大笑，回答道：「遵命，小姐。」他褐色的眼睛閃著光。

P. 81

他們安靜地坐了一會，各自想著自己的心事。茉莉知道，她會想念他。在他住院的這二十六天裡，除了某一天之外，她天天都來探訪他。兩個星期前，當足球隊的巴士從紐約州北部的比賽返回的途中拋描時，她改而打電話給他。

「你還想念她嗎？」雷夫突然問。

他們聊過很多事：雷夫在尼基堤的家鄉，他在那所見的愛琴海景色；雷夫的房子；茉莉的爸爸；她的足球隊；她教練的戰術；還有她的朋友。而他們聊的最少的，是茉莉的媽媽和雷夫的太太。

茉莉不用問「她」是誰。她點點頭。

「你那時幾歲？」他問

「快要十四歲，她在我生日的前兩天去世。」茉莉答道。

「那不容易，我是指悲傷。一開始，根本沒辦法。你懂嗎？」

茉莉又點點頭。

「但慢慢地，美好的事情，那個人讓你愛著的那些事情，填補了空虛。最終，我們會覺得……」他停下來，想找出最恰當的字眼。

「感激？」茉莉探詢。

P. 82

「是的，感激。就是這樣，茉莉。我們覺得感激，因為我們認識了那個人。你看，一切都會結束，茉莉，但祕訣在於，當我們擁有時，欣賞我們所擁有的事物。」

「你的感覺一直是那樣嗎？」茉莉問：「我是説，感激凱莉絲？」

雷夫笑起來，「我過了好久也才明白，太久了。有些人立刻就明白了，有些人要比較久……」

茉莉想到爸爸。她不知道，他是否有像雷夫一樣……像她一樣的感覺。

悲傷
- 曾有你生命中重要的人去世嗎？
- 你的感覺是什麼？告訴朋友。

「但聽著，我們不要傷心。」雷夫説，他的臉上又露出笑容，「我們在這裡，我們很健康，而且我們有朋友和家人。」

「哈囉，你們兩個！」艾芙琳醫師説，走進房間。

雷夫轉過身去，「醫師！歡迎，茉莉和我剛剛正在聊天。」

P. 84

艾芙琳醫師露出微笑，「有些事永遠不會變，」她説，對茉莉眨眨眼：「你的肺快沒力了喔，安朱亞先生。」

雷夫大笑，「別擔心，醫師，它們還很強壯。」

艾芙琳醫師微笑，在掛在病床尾端的病歷上簽名。

「那麼，要回希臘了嗎？」她問，把一綹深色的長髮，從臉上撥開。

「是的，回老家，」雷夫回答道：「我有個哥哥在尼基堤，有姪女和姪子，還有一間我想買的房子。我哥哥和我有艘小船。我們會捕魚，把漁獲賣掉。你一定要來，醫師，你和茉莉。」

在艾芙琳醫師開口前，助理員推著一台輪椅，走進了房間。

「啊，你的車來了。」艾芙琳醫師説。

雷夫搖著頭，坐上輪椅。

艾芙琳醫師和雷夫握手，「很高興認識你，安朱亞先生。祝你一切順利，也許將來有一天，我會去尼基堤，誰知道呢？」

14. 「好久了」

P. 85

「那麼，你覺得表演怎麼樣？」茉莉的爸爸問。

他們站在紐約市時代廣場的一個熱狗攤旁邊。茉莉點頭，嚼了一會，嘴裡塞滿熱狗、泡菜和芥末。她吞下去。

「太棒了，」她説：「謝謝你，爸。這是有史以上最好的生日禮物了。」

他們剛剛去百老匯看了場表演，那是給茉莉的生日驚喜。爸爸那天早上把票給了她，真是慶祝她十七歲生日的好方法！

他們沿百老匯大道走向哥倫布圓環。他們兩人都注意到，有一家餐廳外面掛著希臘國旗。茉莉在他們走過去時，凝視著它，爸爸也在看。他們沒說話，但兩人都記起一年前的那一天。

「你看起來累了，」爸爸終於說：「你想搭計程車嗎？」

P. 87

茉莉點頭。他們停下來，朝著迎面而來的車流。

「雷夫好嗎？」爸爸問，舉起手臂，看著三輛黃色計程車快速開過去。

雷夫返回美國，在信天翁號船長和船員的案子裡作證。在判決確定，船員被關進監獄後，他曾到黑文來，和他們共度了幾天。茉莉和他繼續藉著電子郵件和卡片保持聯絡。

「他很好，」茉莉回道：「他和他哥哥剛買了一艘比較大的船，他們叫它……」

「茉莉？」爸爸問，眼睛看著車流。

茉莉微笑，說道：「凱莉絲。」

就在這時，一輛黃色計程車急速轉彎，停在他們旁邊。

「河濱道，西九十一街，」爸爸從打開的車窗向內說。

計程車司機點點頭。

茉莉和爸爸上了車，計程車快速開走，再次進入車流中。他們要去茉莉的外公、外婆的公寓。自從她母親過世後，到現在已經三年了，這是她和爸爸第一次去他家住。

P. 88

茉莉看著爸爸的臉，認定他看起來很累，也許還有點緊張。

她知道，對爸爸來說，回到外公、外婆的公寓，記起她的母親，這是很痛苦的。但記得她是好的，而且她永遠不會忘記雷夫的忠告：要感激。

茉莉拉起爸爸的手，捏了捏。

爸爸轉過頭來對她笑了笑，問道：「怎麼了？」

「謝謝，謝謝所有的事，爸。」茉莉只是如此說道。

計程車停下來，爸爸付了車錢。

「兩位，晚上愉快。」計程車司機笑著說。

在車外，茉莉和爸爸手挽著手，在那棟高大的公寓大樓外暫停下來。

「好久了……」爸爸說。他抬頭往上看，茉莉也往上看。

一盞接一盞，像星星閃耀一般，來自一千個房間的燈光，在他們的眼前點亮。

爸爸做了個深呼吸，茉莉對他笑了笑，然後兩人一起舉步往前走。

ANSWER KEY

Before Reading

Pages 6-7

1 a) deck   b) hold   c) galley
   d) stairwell   e) hull

2
captain: the leader, the person who is
   at the head of others
crew: the group of sailors in a ship
engineer: member specially trained in
   the construction and use of engines
   and machines
3 An albatross is a large, web-footed
   sea bird.

Pages 8-9

4
a) 1) sixteen 2) Haven 3) Pip
   4) soccer 5) Police 6) two
   7) afternoon 8) crazy
b) 1) Levy 2) sixty-five 3) engineer
   4) retire 5) Greece 6) brother
c) 1) prison 2) work
   3) engineer 4) ship
d) 1) Dan 2) four 3) Shell
   4) widower 5) years

Pages 10-11

5 a) Molly   b) Molly   c) Carlos
   d) Andre   e) Levy   f) Molly
   g) Carlos   h) Andre

6
All: lean, rush, dash
Part: nod, glance, shrug, swallow, wink
Both: step, tighten, sprint

7 (Possible Answer)
a) I would rush. I would step fast,
   I would sprint.
b) I would nod. I would wink.
c) I would glance.
d) I would swallow.
e) I would shrug.
f) I would wink.
8 a) stepped   b) nodded
   c) swallow   d) sprinted

Page 30

* She sees the bird and the ship. She
  finds the watch and a man lying
  against the side of the tree trunk.

Page 50

* They are watching the falcon.
* SWAT is the acronym for "Special
  Weapons And Tactics," which is a law
  enforcement unit, that uses military-
  style light weapons and specialized
  tactics in high-risk operations.

Page 64

* He discovered the falcon in the ship,
  so Carlos and Andre threw him into
  the sea.

After Reading

Page 91

2 a) F b) F c) T d) T e) F
f) T g) F h) T i) T

3
a) Levy was an engineer.
b) He planned to retire and live in Greece.
e) Andre and Carlos threw Levy into the sea.
g) Molly found the watch.

Pages 92-93

4 a) S b) L c) L d) L e) S
5 a) 7 b) 4 c) 2 d) 6
e) 8 f) 1 g) 5 h) 3
6 a) 50 b) 40th c) Herman
d) 40 e) 7 e) 1:38

Pages 94-95

7 a) M b) M c) H d) L e) H
f) L g) L h) H i) M
8 a) Hopper.
b) Molly.
c) Carlos.
d) Andre.
e) Dan Mundy.
f) Carlos.

Pages 96-97

9
a) Carlos, violent
b) The captain, greedy
c) Levy, strong
d) Andre, unintelligent
e) Molly, resourceful
11 a) 5 b) 1 c) 3 d) 2
e) 6 f) 8 g) 7 h) 4
12
a) Andre was always leaving apple cores lying around.
b) It was a present from Levy's wife.
c) Molly recognized Carlos because his shoes had no laces.

Pages 100-101

16
a) Who was Levy's watch found by?
It was found by Molly.
b) When were the falcons discovered?
They were discovered when Levy was looking for Herman.
c) Why were the falcons smuggled?
Because they were rare birds.
d) How many times was Levy nearly killed by Carlos?
Twice.
e) What was Carlos' face covered by in the hospital corridor?
It was covered by flowers.

17
a) Lieutenant Mundy asked the captain what was the new engineer's name. He said that it was Leveros Andreas, but everyone called him Levy.
b) Lieutenant Mundy asked the doctor if he had said anything since he had come in. She answered that he had been unconscious the whole time.

18 a) 3   b) 1   c) 5   d) 2   e) 4

Pages 102-103

19
a) it will mean trouble for all of us.
b) we will spend the next 20 years in prison.
c) I will go to Marty's.
d) then he is lucky.
e) I would drop that pillow and move away from it.

20 a) told
b) had fought; threw
c) woke; got; felt
d) was; saw
e) began; barked
f) found; lay

Test

Pages 104-105

1 a) 1   b) 2   c) 3   d) 2   e) 3
2 a) Cargo ship
b) the captain
c) Carlos
d) Andre
e) Leveros Andreas
f) 2:40 p.m.
g) 815 TVs
h) 60 falcons
3 See page 6, Exercise 1.

Project Work

Page 108

1 lives, birds, nests, number, illegally, beautiful

國家圖書館出版品預行編目資料

信天翁號上的獵鷹 (寂天雲隨身聽APP版) / Scott
Lauder and Walter McGregor 著；蔡裴驊 譯. 一
初版. 一[臺北市]：寂天文化, 2022.08 面；公分.
中英對照; 譯自：The Albatross

ISBN 978-626-300-146-6 (25K平裝)
1.CST: 英語 2.CST: 讀本

805.18   111011745

作者 _ Scott Lauder and Walter McGregor
譯者 _ 蔡裴驊
校對 _ 陳慧莉
製程管理 _ 洪巧玲
出版者 _ 寂天文化事業股份有限公司
發行人 _ 黃朝萍
電話 _ +886-2-2365-9739
傳真 _ +886-2-2365-9835
網址 _ www.icosmos.com.tw
讀者服務 _ onlineservice@icosmos.com.tw
出版日期 _ 2022年8月 初版二刷（寂天雲隨身聽APP版）
郵撥帳號 _ 1998620-0 寂天文化事業股份有限公司
訂書金額未滿1000元，請外加運費100元。
〔若有破損，請寄回更換，謝謝〕

〔限臺灣銷售〕
Copyright © HELBLING LANGUAGES 2016
This edition has been translated and published
under licence from HELBLING LANGUAGES.
For sale in Taiwan only.
Chinese complex characters translation rights
© 2022 by Cosmos Culture Ltd.
All Rights Reserved.